# SKELETON KEYS

## THE NIGHT OF
## THE NOBODY

To Christopher Gatsinzi Simpson and
Elliott Gatsinzi Harris ~ Guy Bass

To you, dear reader! ~ Pete Williamson

STRIPES PUBLISHING LIMITED

An imprint of the Little Tiger Group
1 Coda Studios, 189 Munster Road,
London SW6 6AW

Imported into the EEA by Penguin Random House Ireland,
Morrison Chambers, 32 Nassau Street, Dublin D02 YH68

A paperback original
First published in Great Britain in 2021

Text copyright © Guy Bass, 2021
Illustrations copyright © Pete Williamson, 2021
ISBN: 978-1-78895-335-1

The Fores...                                                    ...ion
dedica...                                                          .
FSC® define...                                                ...rdship
that a... ...upported by...                                ...older...

# SKELETON KEYS

## THE NIGHT OF
# THE NOBODY

WRITTEN BY
## GUY BASS

ILLUSTRATED BY
## PETE WILLIAMSON

# LiTTLE TiGER
### LONDON

The Key to
Reality

The Key to
Second Sight

The Key to
Doorminion

The Forbidden Key

The Key to Time

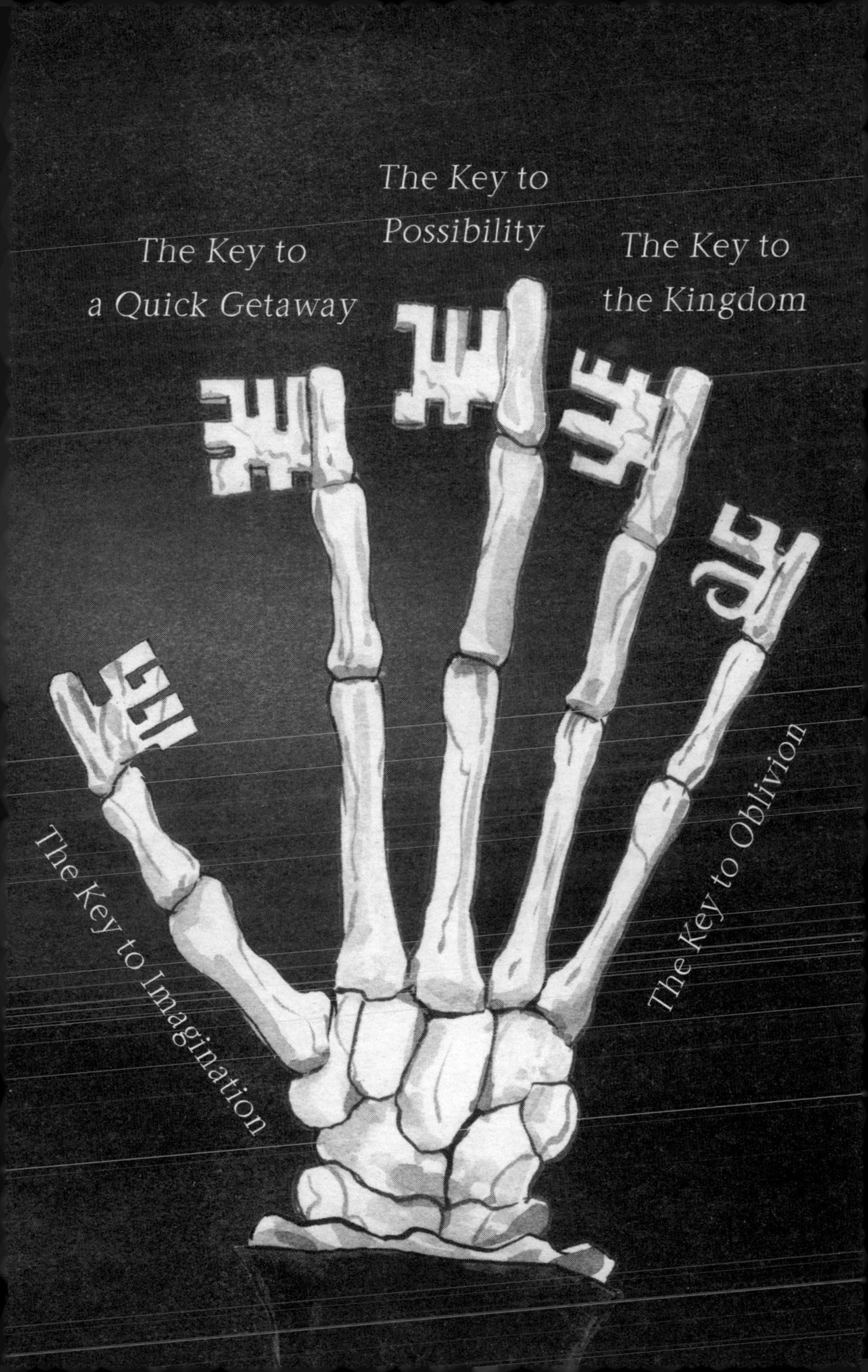
The Key to
Possibility
The Key to
a Quick Getaway
The Key to
the Kingdom
The Key to Imagination
The Key to Oblivion

Greetings! To gadarounds, chanternuts and rooklers! To the imaginary and the unimaginary! To the living, the dead and everyone in between, my name is Keys ... Skeleton Keys.

Hundreds of moons ago, I was an IF – an imaginary friend. Then, before I could say "Crumcrinkles", I was suddenly as real as feet! I had become *unimaginary*.

Now, Ol' Mr Keys looks out for other IFs who find themselves suddenly *unimagined*, whenever, wherever and whyever! For these fantabulant fingers open doors to anywhere and elsewhere ... hidden worlds ... secret places ... doors to the limitless realm of all imagination.

These keys have led me to a hundred adventures and a hundred more relatively soon afterwards! The stories I could tell you...

But of course, it is a *story* you are waiting

for! Well, fret not, dallywanglers – today's
tall tale is such a hum-dum-dinger that it
will make you question the unquestionable.
A tale so truly unbelievable that it must,
unbelievably, be true.

This is Flynn Twist. It is safe to say, which
I do, that Flynn lives in a world of his own.
Even he is not sure why he so often escapes
into his imagination. But, wherever possible,
Flynn lets his mind wander far and wide to
the wonderfilled
world of
his wild
imaginings,
in which
he is the
hero of his
own stories.
They are tales
of a brave

and valiant champion and his mighty steed
... of noble quests and dangers untold ... of a
magical world where anything can happen.

But, little does Flynn know, his life is about
to become stranger and more adventuresome
than he ever could have dreamed.

For strange things can happen when
imaginations run wild...

Our story begins in the quiet, oh-so
slumberly village of Matching Trousers,
population three hundred and forty-three.
It is autumn, and ruddy-reddish leaves strew
quiet, tree-lined streets. Flynn and his infant
sister Nellie have recently moved to Matching
Trousers to live with their grandmother. It
is the end of their first week in the village
and life, though generally uneventful, is not
without surprises...

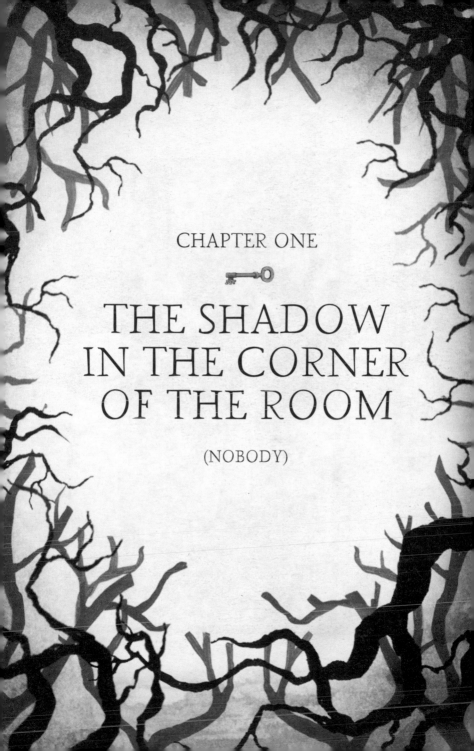

CHAPTER ONE

# THE SHADOW IN THE CORNER OF THE ROOM

## (NOBODY)

*"Adventure awaits! I can feel it in my bones."*

—*SK*

# Ruff Uff RARFF!

Flynn raced back into the house and slammed the front door shut. Next door's dog kept barking. Flynn was quite sure that, given half a chance, that dog would eat him, shoes and all.

"Did you put the bins out?" called his gran from the kitchen.

"He's out there..." Flynn replied. "He's *always* out there."

"Who, Rocky Two?" said Gran. "That dog's bark is worse than his bite ... although his bite could take your head off."

"No, I mean the boy over the road – he's out there again." Flynn edged over to the front window and peered out through a tiny gap in the curtains. The grey gloom of evening had fallen over the village. Still, he could make out the boy standing outside his house on the other side of the road. He was younger than Flynn, maybe five or six, and so bone-thin and pale that he looked altogether unwell. "He's not moving," Flynn added. "He's just standing there, staring."

"There's no crime in standing or staring," said Flynn's gran, coming in from the kitchen with two plates of food. "You'll get used to it."

"I never see anybody else there, but he can't live on his own, it's not allowed," said Flynn. "He's *weird*."

"That's not a crime either, lucky for me," added Gran. Flynn turned to see her with a carrot up each nostril and let out a chuckle. Gran took the carrots out of her nose and put them straight back on their plates. Flynn winced. "Eat, or it'll go cold," she said, taking out her false teeth and dropping them into a glass before tucking in. Flynn winced again and made his way to the dinner table.

All Gran's dinners looked the same – a grey piece of meat surrounded by mushy vegetables, with a comforting, school dinner-ish smell. Not for the first time, Flynn cut the piece of meat in two and, when his gran

wasn't looking, slipped half into his pocket.
If he was to survive tomorrow's encounter
with next door's dog, he would need all the
help he could get.

Flynn's first forkful was heading towards
his mouth when the sound of his sister's
cries echoed through the house. Flynn's gran
looked over at the old grandfather clock, tick-
tocking loudly in the corner of the room.

"She's only been down half an hour," Gran
sighed, taking a mouthful of food. "Nellie does
so hate being left alone. Sounds like she could
do with another one of her brother's stories..."

"I already told her a story," said Flynn. "It
was a new one, too."

"A new tale from Twist World?" said Gran,
taking another mouthful. "What did you call
this one?"

"*Sir Flynnian versus the Horrible Darkness,*"
replied Flynn proudly.

"Charming!" laughed his gran. "Well, I bet she'd love to hear another one – there's nothing Nellie Twist loves more than the adventures of Sir Flynnian and Christopher..."

"*Crystal Fur*," Flynn corrected her. "She's Sir Flynnian's mighty steed."

More mewling came from upstairs. Gran made a deliberate grunt and a show of trying to get up.

"Curse my old bones," she groaned. "By the time I drag myself up those stairs, she'll think nobody's coming..."

"I'll go," said Flynn with an eye-rolling smile as he hopped down from the table. "But you're washing up."

He headed upstairs. Flynn didn't mind delaying his dinner too much – his sister was the only person who seemed to have time for his stories. When she couldn't sleep, he would regale her with tales of his imagined adventures in Twist World. It was a world of Flynn's own creation, in which he was the brave and selfless Sir Flynnian, champion of the Five Islands, who, together with his gleaming light-dragon, Crystal Fur, protected their world against the forces of evil. Sir Flynnian and his mighty steed had saved Twist World a dozen times, with each daring rescue more impressively heroic than the last.

Flynn wasn't sure why his stories settled his sister, but he enjoyed telling them. By the time he'd reached the landing, he'd already decided to tell his sister a sequel to *Sir Flynnian versus the Horrible Darkness*, aptly titled *Sir Flynnian and the Return of the Horrible Darkness*.

"The Horrible Darkness had returned to Twist World..." Flynn began as he pushed open the door to his sister's bedroom.

The room was ice-cold.

A motorized lamp sent a dim rainbow of colours spinning across the ceiling and down to the open window. Curtains shuddered against the incoming breeze. Flynn turned towards his sister to find her standing up in her cot, staring intently into the darkest corner of the room.

"Nellie? You OK?" Flynn asked.

His sister did not move. "No," she replied.

"What's the matter? Did you poo again?" asked Flynn. He went over to the cot and cautiously sniffed the air. "How do you eat nothing and poo everything?"

Nellie raised her tiny arm and pointed in the direction of her stare.

"No," she said again.

Even with the big light off, Flynn couldn't understand why that corner was so dark. It was as if there was an extra shadow there, adding to the gloom.

"It's OK," Flynn said, not that Nellie seemed nervous. "There's … nothing there."

*Is there something there?* he thought. After only a week of living at his gran's, his sister's room was still not entirely familiar. Did Gran keep something in the corner? He squinted at the darkness. The shadow seemed to stir and shift – it was *moving*. What was it? Flynn took two sidesteps towards the door without taking

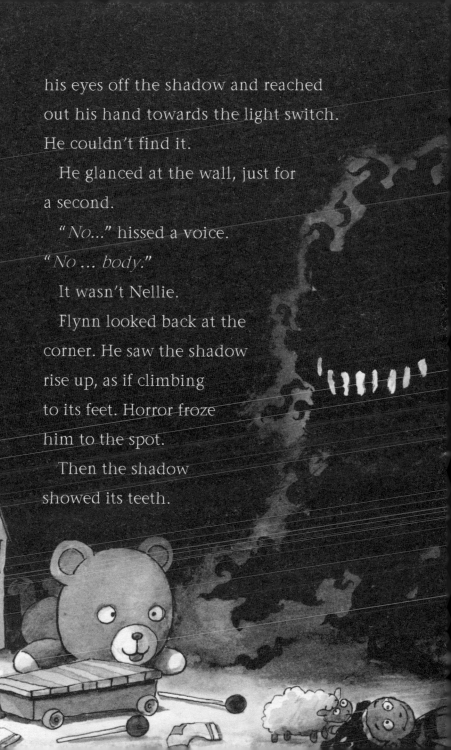

his eyes off the shadow and reached
out his hand towards the light switch.
He couldn't find it.

He glanced at the wall, just for
a second.

"*No...*" hissed a voice.
"*No ... body.*"

It wasn't Nellie.

Flynn looked back at the
corner. He saw the shadow
rise up, as if climbing
to its feet. Horror froze
him to the spot.

Then the shadow
showed its teeth.

# CHAPTER TWO

# FUR

## (FLYNN'S IMAGINARY FRIEND)

*"We have nothing to fear but fear itself.*
*And, of course, monsters."*
*—SK*

T he shadow's teeth seemed to glow in the darkness.

It was *alive*.

It rose up and slid across the room, an almost-human thing. Then it swept towards Nellie's cot and loomed over it.

"No ... *body*," the shadow said again, its voice a low, rasping whisper. A thick cloud of smoky blackness billowed out from the shadow's open mouth. Nellie stared up, her eyes wider than ever.

Flynn had always wondered if, faced with

perils unknown, he could be as brave as his
alter ego, Sir Flynnian. But fear fixed him fast
as the shadow reached for his sister. He tried to
cry out but even that would not come.

*Help*, he thought. Then:

YAP!

# YIP YAP!

The shadow suddenly lurched backwards.
From out of nowhere, something – a *creature*
– had landed on one edge of the cot. For a
horrified moment Flynn thought it was next
door's dog, but the thing on the cot was no
bigger than a cat. The shadow replied to the
creature's barks with a loud hiss and gnashed
its teeth.

As he fumbled breathlessly in the dark,
Flynn finally found the light switch. He
slammed his palm against it. The shadow
let out a grating shriek as stark light filled
the room. It shrank swiftly away before

seeming to pour itself out of the open window. And with that, it disappeared into the darkness.

Flynn raced for the window and slammed it shut. He pressed his face against the glass to see if the shadow was still out there. After a moment he spotted the boy over the road, still standing in his front garden ... still staring up at the house.

*Did he see the shadow?* Flynn thought. *What if it goes after him?*

He was about to call out to the boy when he remembered his sister – and the thing on the edge of her cot.

"Nellie...?" he blurted, spinning round. Nellie was gazing up at the creature, which stood protectively over her.

Flynn recognized it immediately.

He was looking at a figment of his own imagination.

"*Fur?*"

She looked the same as she had in his
imagination – small and four-legged, with
grey fur, an otter-like head and a tufted tail
twice as long as her body. A thin pair of
antennae protruded from Fur's head and a
pair of feathered wings grew from her back.
Flynn blinked hard. "Fur? Is that—?"

"Right, what's all this noi— aaAH!"
shrieked Gran, stepping into the bedroom.
With a startled yelp, the creature jumped off
the edge of the cot and raced under Flynn's
legs. In a single, bounding leap, Fur soared over
Gran's head and out of the doorway.

"Fur!" Flynn said, racing past his gran.
"Gran, get Nellie!"

"What *is* that?" Gran howled, spinning
on her heels as the creature darted down
the stairs.

"It – it's Fur!" Flynn cried, barrelling
downstairs after her. "Crystal Fur!"

"Christopher...?" said Gran as she lifted
Nellie out of the cot.

"Kiss-a-fuh!" Nellie squealed.

Flynn nearly fell down the last few stairs
and tumbled into the living room.

"Fur...?" he puffed, his eyes darting round
the room. As he crept slowly towards the

kitchen, he heard something – a soft, shivery panting – coming from under the table.

Fur's long tail stuck out from beneath it, swishing nervously from left to right. Flynn kneeled down and peered between two chairs. Sure enough, there was the figment of his imagination, huddled and shaking. "It's OK," he whispered. "It's me. It's—"

"Flynn Gatsinzi Twist!" Gran called as she hobbled downstairs with Nellie cradled in her arms. "Are you trying to give me another heart attack 'cause let me tell you they're no picnic, and I don't even like picnics..."

"Gran, *shhh*...!" said Flynn, his finger pressed to his lips. "You'll *scare* her."

After a moment, the tiny, grey-furred creature emerged from beneath the table and peered up at Gran.

"Well, I'll be a monkey's underwear," Gran said with a shake of her head. "I had a feeling this might happen sooner or later."

"How...?" whispered Flynn, holding his hand out. Fur sniffed it and her antennae pressed contentedly against her head. Flynn sat back and folded his legs, and the little creature climbed on to his lap, purring gently. "It's really her," he whispered, stroking the top of Fur's head. "From Twist World."

"From your imagination," his gran said. "You've done it now, *Sir Flynnian*. He's coming."

"He, who?" asked Flynn. The answer came a moment later, in the form of a

KNOCK

  KNOCK

    KNOCK at the door.

# CHAPTER THREE

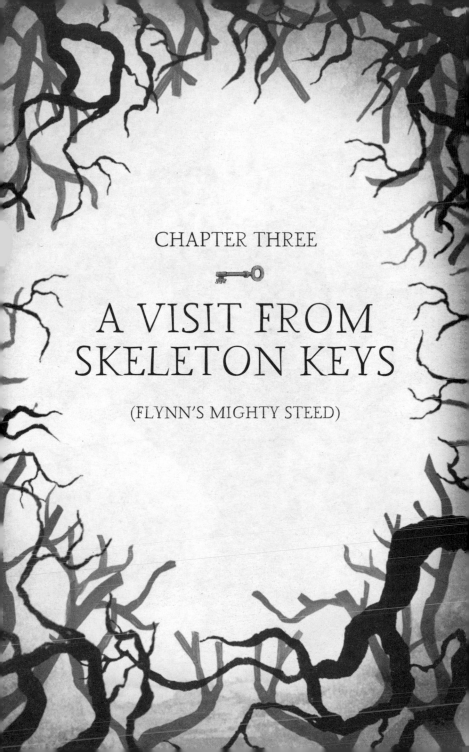

# A VISIT FROM SKELETON KEYS

## (FLYNN'S MIGHTY STEED)

*From The Important Thoughts of Mr S. Keys*
*Volume 12: Doors*

*Now you are here and then you are there*
*For a door may lead you anywhere!*

Flynn heard the
CLICK
CLUNK
of a key turning in the front door.

"Right on cue," said Gran with a sigh.
A gust of air swept into the room as the door
swung on its hinges. Flynn's gasp disappeared
down his throat.

In the doorway stood a skeleton dressed in
a tailcoat.

"The problem with going out after dark,"
the skeleton began, doffing his three-peaked

hat with a bow, "is you never know *who* you are going to meet."

"Gran, RUN!" Flynn screamed, leaping to his feet as Fur barked wildly.

"Run, with *my* knees? You'll be lucky," Gran tutted. "Put your panic in a pot, Flynn – I know Mr Keys of old."

"Kn-know him?" Flynn stuttered as the skeleton glared at him through milk-white eyeballs.

"And rather hoped I'd never see him again," continued his gran, putting Nellie into her high chair. "Thank you for coming, Mr Keys … but there's nothing to concern you here."

"Grinnering to see you too, Dilys Twist!" the skeleton said as Fur sniffed his shoe. "How long has it been since my last visit to Matching Trousers?"

"Not long enough," said Flynn's gran. "I see you haven't changed a bit."

"Skinless is how I came into this world, and so skinless is how I remain," replied the skeleton with a shrug. "Meanwhile, you have grown most impressively crease-faced and crinkled!"

"I *meant* you're still sticking your keys in other folk's business," Gran huffed.

"I assure you, madam, Ol' Mr Keys and his fantabulant fingers only appear when needed," replied the skeleton, sweeping his hands dramatically through the air. Flynn noticed that each of the skeleton's fingers was tipped with a bone key, as if they had grown that way.

"G-Gran, what's going on?" Flynn muttered, picking up Fur from the floor and edging towards the table. His gran rubbed her eyes.

"May I present Mr Keys," she said. "Mr Keys, my family. This is Flynn, and the little stink bomb is Nellie."

"Nee-Nee!" said Nellie, trying to say her own name.

"I do declare, ankle-sprouts get smaller by the day," Skeleton Keys noted as he stared at her. Nellie poked the skeleton on the chin, before he turned to Flynn. "But 'twas not she who gave me the *twitch*."

"The – the twitch?" Flynn repeated. Skeleton Keys held out a key-tipped finger to Fur. After a cautious sniff, she seemed to relax and gave the key a casual nibble.

"There was I, at home in my Doorminion, when the twitch came upon me," continued Skeleton Keys. "It led me to your door, for that most profound rattle of the bones can mean one thing and one thing alone..."

"An *unimagining*," said Gran.

"A what?" asked Flynn.

"Exactly! An unimagining!" repeated Skeleton Keys, prising his finger out of Fur's mouth. "A figment of wild imagination, suddenly as real as earlobes. *Unimaginary!*"

Flynn repeated the word in his head. *Unimaginary.* Fur peered up at him and let out a happy yap.

"Well, as you can see, everything's fine," said Gran, gesturing towards the creature in Flynn's arms. "You'll get no bother from Christopher."

"*Crystal Fur,*" Flynn corrected her. "She's my – *Sir Flynnian's* – mighty steed."

"Mighty steed?" repeated Skeleton Keys. "Crumcrinkles, but is she not entirely too small to carry you?"

"This is her *normal form*," said Flynn. He let Fur hop to the floor and held an arm straight above his head. "Her *heroic form* is this big. Bigger."

"... Heroic? Fantabulant! A hero and his mighty steed, united in the bright glare of reality," laughed Skeleton Keys. "Cheese 'n' biscuits! My twitch was so itchy-twitchy that I was *certain* this new unimaginary would be a rottering rugslugger, yet it seems your unimaginary friend is no trouble at all..."

"*But you promised*," said a voice. In that instant, a girl materialized in the middle of the room. She was a deathly grey colour, with wild eyes and a scowl fixed to her face.

And her head was on backwards.

"You promised me trouble, bone-bag," the girl hissed. "Bring me trouble, or I'll make some of my own."

# CHAPTER FOUR

# NOBODY HERE

## (UNCHANGED)

*A peaceful village, plagued by fear*
*A monstrous, dreadish Beast draws near!*
*It prowls the streets! It howls! It growls!*
*Its motives, surely fulsome foul!*
*But then, the beast just disappeared!*
*'Tis most confuddingly weird...*

"May I present my partner-in-problem-solving, Daisy," said Skeleton Keys with a flourish. The girl with the backwards head scowled at Flynn.

"Boo," she said. Flynn instinctively recoiled, stumbling back into the table. He tried to steady himself and ended up putting a hand in his dinner.

"Big baby," Daisy said with a lopsided grin as Flynn wiped his hand on his trousers. "I can turn invisible – what can you do, except wet your pants?"

"Don't be rude, young lady," said Gran, eyeing the girl with the backwards head suspiciously.

"Why not? I like being rude and I'm very good at it," Daisy replied. She glared at Fur, who looked quizzically back at her. "Can we go now, bone-bag? You said this unimaginary was bound to be a *monster* – all I see is this *not-quite-a-cat*."

"She's a dragon," insisted Flynn nervily. "And that's her normal form. Her heroic form is—"

"The question is, who cares? The answer is, shut up," said Daisy, and glowered at Skeleton Keys. "I'm sick of being the scariest person in the room, bone-bag. Where are the really *wild* unimaginaries? You told me last time you came here there was a *beast*."

"Not just any beast – the Beast of Matching Trousers!" declared Skeleton Keys.

"The what?" Flynn asked.

"Let me tell you, it is not every day that Ol' Mr Keys comes face-to-skull with such a monster! Your grandmother has quite the wild imagination, Flynn."

"My gran?" said Flynn. He turned to his gran and saw her expression harden. "You imagin— *un*imagined a monster?"

"It was a long time ago," replied Gran, rubbing her eyes. She already seemed keen to change the subject.

"And *what* a monster!" said Skeleton Keys. "The beast struck chillering fear into the hearts of the unsuspecting villagers as it prowled the lanes and snickets of Matching Trousers."

"Sounds like trouble," said Daisy. "When can I meet it?"

"It's *gone*," said Flynn's gran quickly. "Never to be seen again, thanks to Mr Keys and a small army of proverbial pitchfork-wielding villagers."

"The one that got away..." noted Skeleton Keys, with a rueful tone. "I was hunting the beast when, all of a sudden, it disappeared. I searched for many a long moon – high and low, not to mention far and wide – but it was as though the beast vanished off the face of the earth. A most confuddling conundrum!"

"Life's full of disappointments," said Flynn's gran. "The scariest thing you'll find in Matching Trousers these days is Nellie's bottom-pops."

"Scariest...?" repeated Flynn, the word bringing back his encounter with the shadow. "There – there was something ... a *thing* in Nellie's room. It tried to *get* her. Fur saved her!"

"Thing?" repeated Gran. "What sort of thing?"

"I don't know – like a shadow," Flynn replied, curving his arms over his head. "It was *this* big and it had teeth and black clouds in its mouth and—"

"*Liar*," huffed Daisy. "I checked the whole house when I was invisible. There's nobody else here."

"That's what it said! 'Nobody'," said Flynn. "And then it jumped out of the window. Nellie saw it too! *Tell* them, Nellie."

Nellie let out a little fart. Daisy tutted.

"Keep on lying and your nose will grow, *Flynn-ochio*," she said. "Are you feeling bad 'cause all you can unimagine is your not-cat?"

"I'm *not* lying! There was something there," insisted Flynn defensively. "And Fur's a light-dragon from the Island of Crystal and the mightiest steed in all of Twist World and she can fly and she can breathe actual starlight and she's this big. Bigger!"

"Ugh, I hate *fan fiction*," scoffed Daisy. "Go on then, prove it – change."

Flynn looked at his dragon – and grinned.

"Fine ... but you should probably stand back," he said. Skeleton Keys and Flynn's gran exchanged concerned glances. Daisy rolled her eyes. Flynn couldn't help but swell with pride. After all, he knew what was coming.

"Go on, Fur," he said with a wink. "Show them."

Flynn's dragon peered up at him, her antennae twitching happily. But she did not change. Daisy tutted.

"It's OK, Fur – show them your heroic form," Flynn coaxed. The dragon let out a little belch and a tiny spark of light fizzed out of her mouth and disappeared in an instant.

But she did not change.

"Told you he was lying," said Daisy with a grin. "Now show us the big, scary shadow monster you made up, Flynn-ochio."

"I didn't make it up," Flynn insisted. "And Fur is a light-dragon! I mean, she was in my head..."

"The transition from imaginary to unimaginary can be a flabbergasting affair," said Skeleton Keys. "Perhaps Christopher is discombobulated by her new surroundings. She may not even *remember* who she is." He inserted a key-tipped thumb into the lock on the grandfather-clock door. "Take my hand, ankle-sprout."

"W-what?" stuttered Flynn as the skeleton held out his other hand. He glanced at his gran, who rolled her eyes and gave a nod. Flynn took a deep breath and placed his hand in the skeleton's. Skeleton Keys turned his thumb in the clock with a CLICK CLUNK and pulled open the door.

Instead of the swinging pendulum of a grandfather clock, Flynn was confronted by an impossible sight – five vast islands, floating, suspended in a bright, endless sky.

"Can't be..." he gasped. "*Twist World?*"

"Such is the power of the *Key to Imagination*!" declared Skeleton Keys. "Flynn Twist, gaze upon the realm of your own imagining."

Flynn peered, wide-eyed, inside the clock at his invented world. It was all there – the five great islands of Earth, Air, Fire, Cheese and Fur's home, Crystal, with its vast, shimmering spires.

"I've imagined better," Daisy huffed.

"Fur, look – it's home," said Flynn, adding in a self-conscious whisper, "Remember? You're Crystal Fur, greatest of all the light-dragons."

The little creature scratched an ear with her back leg – but remained well and truly unchanged. Flynn looked round at a room full of expectant faces and sighed.

"I am quite certain Christopher's memory will return in time," said Skeleton Keys, closing the door to the grandfather clock and turning the key with a CLUNK CLICK. "Or not! Such are the fickle-picklings of unimaginary life…"

"This 'adventure' could not be more rubbish," groaned Daisy. "Can't we just unimagine our own monsters, bone-bag?"

"Unimaginaries cannot unimagine, Daisy, everybody knows that," said Skeleton Keys.

"Good job too," said Gran, glowering at Daisy. She ushered Skeleton Keys towards the front door. "As you can see, Mr Keys, our new addition is no trouble at all. Don't let us keep you."

"But – but what about the shadow?" Flynn asked.

"Fret not, ankle-sprout!" said Skeleton Keys. "Ol' Mr Keys is a dab hand at handling the hard-to-handle! In case of danger, just—"

"Flynn doesn't need your help, Mr Keys – he's got me," interrupted Gran as she pulled open the door. Daisy wasted no time in leaving but Skeleton Keys paused in the doorway and turned back.

"Be watchful, Dilys," he said. "This shadow the sprout encountered could be *another* unimaginary. Perhaps I should return in the morning to—"

"Don't," said Gran firmly. She rubbed her eyes again. "I'd rather you didn't add your particular brand of chaos to our lives, thank you very much."

And with that, Flynn's gran slammed the door in the skeleton's face.

CHAPTER FIVE

A HERO'S QUEST

(GETTING PAST ROCKY TWO)

*Real worlds are well and grand*
*But I prefer imagined lands*
*Of all the worlds that I have been*
*None wilder have I ever seen*

After everything that had happened that evening, Flynn did not expect to sleep at all. He thought he'd lie in the dark with his eyes open, thinking of nothing but the madness of the previous night – of the strange, shadowy Nobody ... of the key-fingered skeleton who knocked at their door ... of *unimaginaries*. But with his mighty steed Fur stretched out on his bed, he quickly fell into a deep, dreamless sleep. It was late morning when the pair awoke to the smell of bacon and eggs wafting up the stairs.

They raced each other to the dining table. Nellie was already in her high chair, busily pushing messy globs of porridge into her mouth and seemingly unaffected by the previous night's events.

Gran slid a plateful of breakfast in front of Flynn.

"Oh, who will come to my aid!" she said dramatically. "Only the bravest, noblest hero can undertake my important quest. Where can I find such a fearless champion?"

"What sort of quest...?" asked Flynn as Fur hopped up on to the chair next to him.

"A hero's quest, of course," Gran replied, retrieving a white envelope from the mantelpiece. She licked it and sealed it tight. "I need you to take a very important letter over to Mr Nash at the windmill."

"Old Mr Nash *again*?" The windmill was all the way on the other side of the village. Still,

Flynn never refused a quest. "Can I take Fur?" he added, feeding his unimaginary friend a piece of bacon.

"What sort of a quest would it be if Sir Flynnian didn't have his mighty steed?" replied Gran. "But do me a favour – don't go showing her off. Folk round here don't care for wild imaginations ... or unimaginaries. They see different as dangerous."

"Is that what happened to your – to the Beast of Matching Trousers?" Flynn asked. "Did they think it was dangerous?"

"They were scared," replied Gran with a sigh. "Once folk are scared, it doesn't matter what's real, or what's imagined."

"*Was* the beast scary?" asked Flynn.

"Not to me."

"Do you know where it went?"

Gran narrowed her eyes. "Where no one can get to it," she said. Then she waved the letter and added, "Now get questing, you. This letter won't deliver itself."

Flynn's gran pressed her lips against the envelope, leaving a pink lipstick mark in its corner.

"Eww, Gran! What sort of letter is it?"

"Never you mind," she said, slapping the letter on the table. "Only know that the quest is noble and, with any luck, you'll be babysitting Nellie for me on Friday night."

"Eww!"

Ten minutes later, Flynn took a deep breath of autumn air and stepped out of the front door. Gran's letter was safely stowed in his backpack, along with sandwiches enough to last the day. The quest had begun. As far as Flynn was concerned, he was now *Sir Flynnian of Twist World*. He no longer saw wooden fences and thatched roofs and orderly flowerbeds – he saw the five floating islands of Earth, Air, Fire, Cheese and Crystal that he and his mighty steed were sworn to protect. He could see it as clearly in his head as he did through the door of the grandfather clock.

But this time, he really did have his mighty steed with him – even if she wasn't an enormous, glimmering light-dragon. With Fur by his side, Flynn felt one step closer to being the brave hero of his own imagining. His fear of the shadow was probably a one-off, he thought – next time he was called on to be brave, he was sure he wouldn't hesitate.

"Onward, Fur," he said. "To action, adventure and dangers untol—"

RARF!

RRARFF!

Flynn almost jumped out of his skin. Next door's front gate rattled as the neighbour's dog leaped against it, barking wildly. Flynn thought Rocky Two looked more like a polar bear than a dog – huge and white, with a slavering mouth and gnashing jaws – he was already frantically patting the pockets of his jeans for last night's steak when Fur leaped forwards and let out a high-pitched yap.

"Fur, wait!" Flynn cried but Rocky Two's thunderous barks had already drowned Fur out. Flynn grabbed the slab of meat from his back pocket and flung it over the fence. The dog seemed to swallow it without chewing but it gave Flynn and Fur just enough time to dart past the gate.

"You *sure* you don't want to change into a mighty light-dragon?" he asked Fur as they made their way down the street. "You could squish that dog flat. Plus if we flew we'd be at the windmill in no time..."

Fur gave him a quizzical look. Flynn sighed and glanced back to make sure next door's dog had not somehow broken free and given pursuit. He saw the boy over the road in his front garden, peering at Gran's house. For a moment, Flynn wondered if he was looking for the shadow.

*Is it still here, somewhere?* Flynn thought. He nervously picked up his pace a little but, as he turned the corner, he stopped to glance back and saw the boy leave his garden and cross the road. Flynn squinted.

"Where's he off to?" he whispered to Fur, who was distractedly sniffing a nearby post box. Flynn watched the boy make a beeline for his gran's house. He knocked once and waited. A moment later Gran opened the door.

Then, without pause, the boy over the road stepped inside.

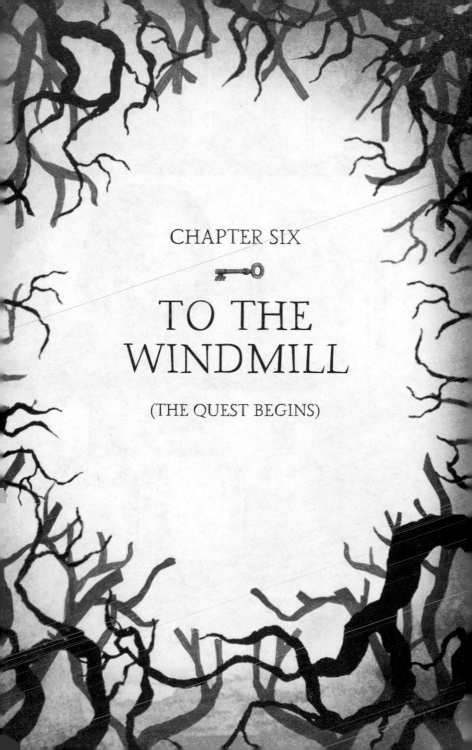

# CHAPTER SIX

# TO THE WINDMILL

## (THE QUEST BEGINS)

*"All the adventures begin in the imagination."*
*—SK*

"Why would the boy over the road go to Gran's?" Flynn said as he and Fur passed by the village shop. "She didn't even ask him what he wanted – she just let him in like she knew he was coming. Why would she know he was coming? I didn't even think she really knew him..."

Fur offered no reply as she trotted alongside him. Flynn peered through the shop window. Inside, beyond jars of invitingly colourful sweets, the shopkeeper, Mrs McCoffey, gave them a wave.

"Mrs McCoffey, can't add for toffee," Flynn muttered. His gran had introduced him to half the village on his first day in Matching Trousers, and created rhymes to help him remember them all – everyone except the boy over the road. He didn't even know the boy's name. His gran had never even introduced them. He suddenly felt like she was keeping secrets from him. It made him feel uneasy and, worse still, unwelcome. Had she only given him a quest to get him out of the house, so she could see the boy over the road?

Suddenly, Fur let out a sharp yap. Flynn realized he'd stopped walking. He glanced down at his dragon to find her peering judgementally up at him, clearly impatient to get on with their quest.

"Right, sorry," he said. He tried his best to put thoughts of his gran and the boy over the road behind him and focus on the matter in hand.

So, on they quested.

By the time they reached the old oak tree, which stood like an ancient monument on the village green, Flynn had decided that his gran's letter was the final part of a powerful spell that Sir Flynnian and Fur must deliver to the ancient Cheese Wizard.

"Without it, the Island of Cheese is doomed," he explained to Fur. The scrappy cawing of a dozen or so crows interrupted his train of thought. Flynn looked up to see the birds perched upon wide-reaching branches among the amber leaves. "Hex witches," he said, narrowing his eyes. "Don't listen, Fur, or they'll take over your brain."

Flynn put his fingers in his ears until they were clear of the crow's bewitching caws. He

and Fur made their way past the church with
its wonky gravestones, past the allotments,
where Doug Dringle was noisily mumbling
nonsense and sniffing himself as he turned
soil with a trowel – ("Doug Dringle, no
wonder he's single") – and then all the way
up Trouser Hill to the windmill. The climb
to the top was steep but worth it. As far as
Flynn was concerned, the windmill was the
best thing about Matching Trousers. Looming
over the horizon with its sails stretched wide,
it looked like a great, white fortress. Today
it was the Citadel of Cheddar, home to the
Great Cheese Wizard – the sort of place a hero
might defend from an invading army, with
the help of a mighty steed, of course.

"We made it," said Flynn as he reached
the windmill, hot and breathless. He took
the letter out of his backpack as Fur sniffed
around near the front door.

"I hope this letter isn't what it looks like," he muttered to himself, staring at the lipstick mark. He pushed the letter into his coat pocket, rang the bell on the wall and waited for Old Mr Nash to come to the door.

Silence. Flynn rang again and waited.

Fur sniffed the air, increasingly agitated.

"Maybe he's not in..." Flynn muttered. He stepped back and looked up and up to the windmill's high windows as the little grey dragon nudged the door with her otter snout.

A CREEEAAK rang out across the hill, and Flynn realized that the door was ajar. Before he knew what was happening, Fur slipped through the narrow gap.

"Wait—" Flynn whispered. His mighty steed seemed to take questing even more seriously than he did. Flynn peeked inside. It was strangely dark. A shiver came with the memory of the shadow in his sister's bedroom. He suddenly felt like running away again – but Fur was already inside.

*Sir Flynnian would finish the quest,* he told himself.

Then he took a deep breath and pushed open the door.

# CHAPTER SEVEN

# NOBODY IS HERE

## (SOMETHING STRANGE ABOUT OLD MR NASH)

*"Even the wildest imagination is a little wilder*
*in the dark."*
—SK

"Fur...?" Flynn whispered as he stepped inside the windmill. The curtains were drawn shut and the lights were off, so it took Flynn a moment to adjust to the darkness. Grey walls curved round Old Mr Nash's sparse front room. In the middle was a small table upon which stood a round fishbowl. Flynn could just make out a single goldfish floating with an eerie stillness in the water. It seemed to be looking right at him.

Then, from the gloom, came a growl. Flynn turned to see Fur outside a doorway at the far end of the room, her hackles up.

"Fur...!" Flynn hissed as he narrowed his eyes. There was someone beyond the doorway, standing in what looked like the kitchen. Even in the darkness, he recognized Old Mr Nash's swirling waves of thick, silver hair. The old man was standing in the middle of the room, motionless. At first Flynn thought he was looking out of the window but the kitchen blinds were pulled down.

"Mr – Mr Nash?" Flynn said softly. He edged a step closer. "Mr Na—?"

# FPPPPT.

A fart.

Old Mr Nash had farted. It was loud enough to make Fur stop growling. Flynn blushed.

"Hello, Flynn," said Old Mr Nash, without turning round. His voice sounded low, flat and blank.

Flynn fumbled inside his coat pocket and

took out the letter. "I, uh, I have this from my gran," he said, waving the letter weakly. Old Mr Nash still did not move. "Should – shall I just leave it here? Mr Nash?"

At last, Old Mr Nash turned to face Flynn. He was just as Flynn remembered him, with a well-combed mass of grey-white hair covering his top lip – ("Old Mr Nash, what a mighty moustache") – but he had a strange, distant look in his eyes. He stared at Flynn as if he was looking through him.

"Old Mr Nash isn't here," he said. "Nobody is here."

"Sorry?" said Flynn.

"I said, *the Nobody* is here," said Old Mr Nash.

The letter fell from Flynn's hand. "W-what?" he whispered, cold, freezing dread returning to his bones.

"*No. Body,*" Old Mr Nash said. "But now

the Nobody is *somebody*. And it's just the beginning. When darkness falls, the Nobody will be here ... there ... everywhere."

Despite his fear, Flynn found himself picking up a still-growling Fur off the floor.

"I – I should go," Flynn whispered, so quietly he barely heard it himself. He backed slowly away towards the front door, not taking his eyes off Old Mr Nash.

"There's no point in running, Flynn – there's no escape," said Old Mr Nash matter-of-factly. "The Nobody will find you soon enough. And not just you. By tomorrow, the Nobody will be—"

*FPP-PT!*

Old Mr Nash's fart echoed round the windmill. "Pardon me," he continued. "By tomorrow, the Nobody will be everybody ... and everybody will be the Nobody."

Then he started to close in.

Flynn spun on his heels and ran. He immediately spotted the goldfish bowl on the table and veered left to avoid it, slamming his shoulder hard against the wall – and accidentally colliding with a light switch. Bright white light flooded the windmill and Old Mr Nash let out a pained wail. Flynn did not look back – he raced out of the windmill and down the other side of Trouser Hill so quickly that he almost fell over. With Fur still in his arms, he ran and ran, down into Trouser Woods.

*He called himself the Nobody*, Flynn thought, his legs burning as he frantically weaved through the ancient trees. It had to be the shadow he encountered in his sister's bedroom – could it have somehow *become* Old Mr Nash? And what did he mean by "everybody will be the Nobody?"

In the densest part of the wood, Flynn dived behind a tall tree and slumped into a pile of fallen leaves. He crouched there with his back pressed up against the gnarled trunk, his heart pounding in his chest, Fur held close. Though he couldn't be sure, he imagined she could only be thinking one thing: *For a mighty hero, you spend a lot of time running away, Flynn Twist.*

"Just ... stay here ... for a bit," he panted. "Get my ... breath back..."

Fur let out a purr and nestled her head into his elbow. Slowly, Flynn's fear began to ebb away.

*Stay here,* he thought. *Stay here, where no one can find me. Stay here, where it's safe.*

And that was when a door appeared in the tree.

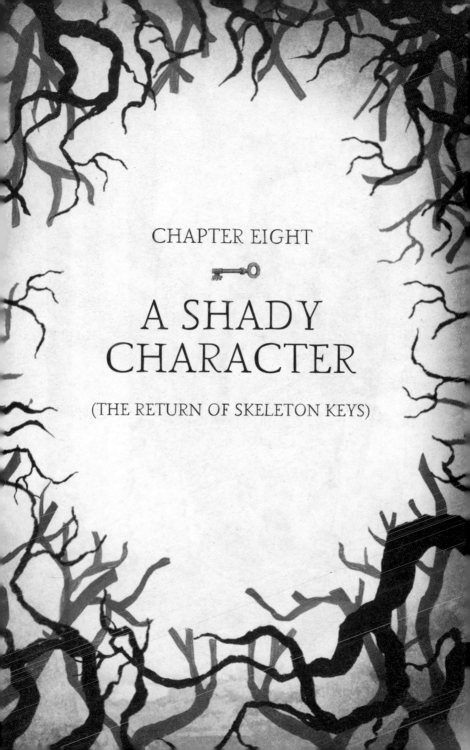

CHAPTER EIGHT

# A SHADY CHARACTER

(THE RETURN OF SKELETON KEYS)

*Somewhere between IFs and unimaginary friends
are Shady Characters. Neither one nor the other,
but somehow, mayhap and flabbergastingly, both.
Confuddled? You should be!*

F lynn didn't see the door materialize in
the tree. It wasn't until it swung open,
shoving him face-first into a pile of fallen
leaves, that he came to the horrifying
realization that they were not alone in the
wood. Fur yapped loudly as Flynn looked
round to see the impossible – an open door in
the tree trunk, as if it had always been there.
Then impossibility heaped upon impossibility
as Skeleton Keys and Daisy stepped out of the
doorway into the woods.

"Dogs 'n' cats, ankle-sprout, there you are!"

cried the skeleton as he strode through. "By my bones, I have opened half the doors in the village and a hundred more out of thinnest air looking for you..."

Flynn stared aghast at the doorway in the tree.

"H-how did you—?"

"Find you? With the *Key to a Quick Getaway*, of course!" the skeleton declared, brandishing one of his key-tipped fingers. "This key can open doors even when there are none! Which is convenient when the ankle-sprout you are looking for is hiding in a dark forest..."

"I – I'm not hiding," said Flynn, glancing guiltily at Fur.

"What are you doing here then?" Daisy said. "Are you on a magic quest to the land of blah-de-blah, or is this where you come to do your best crying?"

"Daisy, I thought we agreed that if you cannot think of something gladdening to say, do not speak – and if that means you spend a month or two in utter silence, then so be it," chided Skeleton Keys, before fixing his gaze upon Flynn. "Sprout, your grandmother may be content that all is well but I have been dealing with unimaginaries since before her mother's mother had a mother. My twitch tells me there is a troublesome unimaginary in Matching Trousers – and my twitch is never wrong."

"Pfff, what about that time with the mermaid?" said Daisy. "Or the time with the giant ant-thingy? Or the time we chased that unimaginary fox for two days and it turned out it was just a fox? Or the time—"

"Cheese 'n' biscuits, Daisy, focus!" Skeleton Keys interrupted. "We must deal with the unimaginary in hand. Something is not right with—"

"—Old Mr Nash," Flynn interrupted.

"Who?" asked the skeleton.

"Something's wrong with Old Mr Nash at the windmill," said Flynn. "He's my gran's... They're sort of – actually, I don't know what's going on and I don't want to, but I was just there at the windmill and it was dark and he wasn't... There was something not right about him. He said 'Nobody', like the shadow in Nellie's room. He said everybody will be the Nobody and the Nobody will be everybody."

"So what? He's old. Old people say stupid stuff," said Daisy.

"What happened then, sprout?" Skeleton Keys asked Flynn.

"I – I ran," Flynn confessed, glancing shamefully at Fur.

"You ran away from an old man?" Daisy sneered. "You're just as heroic as you look, *Run-a-Wayne*."

Skeleton Keys tapped his chin with his key-tipped fingers. "No ... *body*. I wonder, is it possible? Could it be? If there is even the slim-slightest chance that—"

"*What*?" Daisy spat out the word.

"Why, it could be a *Shady Character*," Skeleton Keys exclaimed. "They are rarer than a skeleton with a stomach but..."

"What's a 'shady character'?" asked Flynn.

"An unimaginary without true form," Skeleton Keys explained. "Once in a blue-hued moon an IF enters the real world without completely crossing over from the realm of the imagined. As a result, it is neither truly imaginary nor entirely real. A Shady Character tends to fear the light, since it is in *darkness* where the imagined appears most real – but it will stop at nothing to find a true, physical form ... a body of its own."

"Old Mr Nash!" Flynn exclaimed. "He said that now the Nobody is *somebody*."

"Let us suppose this Shady Character found its way through your sister's window to possess her and become completely real," Skeleton Keys mused. He spun towards Flynn and looked him square in the eyes. "But then, lo and below, *you* appeared and bravely faced the fiercing foe, unimagining your own IF, Christopher, to aid you in your noble plight—"

"To save him, more like," interrupted Daisy.

"The Shady Character – the Nobody – fled," continued the skeleton, revelling in his deductive prowess. "Having failed to claim your sister, the Nobody made its way through the darkness in search of another poor soul – and found its victim at the windmill."

"Old Mr Nash…" Flynn whispered. "He said when darkness falls the Nobody will be here and there and everywhere."

"Dogs 'n' cats!" Skeleton Keys uttered, striding up and down as he rubbed his chin with his key-tipped fingers. "Perhaps this Nobody is not content with *one* form – perhaps it seeks to possess yet more victims.

Imagine, a single mind, keen to conquer countless bodies, spreading like fungus or falsehoods or fear!"

"So, this thing is real?" said Daisy. "You might have actually done something right, *Peter Pant-wetter*."

"What do you mean?" asked Flynn.

"I mean, if you unimagined an evil shadow monster, we might finally see some *touble*," Daisy replied with a lopsided grin.

"Me? I didn't unimagine the Nobody!"
Flynn protested.

"Of course you did – you were trying to
unimagine your not-cat and something else
popped out of your brain at the same time,"
said Daisy, sneering at Fur. "All the really
*dangerous* IFs are unimagined by accident.
I should know – I'm one of them."

"But I didn't! Did I?" muttered Flynn,
hardly daring to entertain the idea. He didn't
exactly keep track of all his thoughts but
surely he couldn't have unimagined the
Nobody if he didn't remember imagining it
in the first place?

Then another thought struck him so hard it
took his breath away. The bedroom window
was open when he first encountered the
Nobody. And when he closed the window and
looked out, he saw him:

"The boy over the road!" Flynn blurted.

"Last night, he was there. He was watching the house when the Nobody appeared."

"Maybe he saw you crying and wanted to give you a hanky," said Daisy.

"Daisy!" snapped Skeleton Keys. He spun on his bony heels and came face to face with Flynn. "If you did not unimagine this Nobody, ankle-sprout, then someone else did. The plot thickens with soupy speed! Still, we must begin with young Mr Nash at the windmill..."

"What should I do?"

"Not a thing! Except, fret not," said Skeleton Keys, striding back towards the tree-trunk doorway. "Ol' Mr Keys is on the case!"

"Maybe you should go home and hide under the bed, scaredy-coward," said Daisy, eyeballing Flynn as the skeleton disappeared. "Make-believe just got *real*."

With that, she walked through the

doorway, her back-to-front head still staring at him, and pulled the door shut.

Flynn breathed a sigh of relief.

He looked down at Fur and the pair of them stood there for a moment in silence, listening to the wind singing through the trees, coaxing autumn leaves from their branches.

Then Flynn heard another sound, faint and far away, carried on a distant wind ... a sound that chilled him to the core.

A fart.

# CHAPTER NINE

# TWIST WORLD

## (DARKNESS FALLS)

"A horse may aid your journey
A boat can take you home
But a story will transport you
To where e'er you wish to go!"
—SK

Flynn did not go home.

He knew he should probably check on Nellie and his gran and, if he was feeling up to it, confront Gran about her secret association with the boy over the road. After all, if there was a chance that the boy unimagined the Nobody, wasn't he the most important part of the puzzle?

But Flynn had never been a fan of facing up to reality, especially the uncomfortable possibility that his gran was keeping things from him. Instead, with his mighty steed by his side, Flynn drifted into his own imagination ... and Twist World.

He and Fur spent the day wandering the outskirts of Matching Trousers (or rather, patrolling the lawless badlands on the outer reaches of the Island of Cheese), before settling in a bus shelter (hidden cheese cave) to eat their cheese sandwiches (which, since cheese sandwiches could not be improved upon, were still cheese sandwiches).

With his belly full and little desire to go home, Flynn leaned out of the shelter and peered up at the low, darkening clouds.

"When you look at the sky, you could be anywhere," he said. Fur yapped, as if in agreement. Flynn wondered if a story might help to remind her who she was. After all, to him they were just tales but to his unimaginary friend, all of their adventures had been real. "Further than the furthest away star in the sky," he began, "there is a place called Twist World."

The story Flynn told in the bus shelter was the same tale he'd told his sister only yesterday – *Sir Flynnian versus the Horrible Darkness*. It was filled with heroes, villains, impossible odds and wild adventure in all five of Twist World's magical islands. By the time the story reached its dramatic conclusion, the sun had started to set.

"... The Horrible Darkness spread across Twist World. It got everybody. It took them over, until nobody was left," said Flynn, getting to his feet. "Except Sir Flynnian and Fur, who didn't get got. They fought past everyone on the Five Islands until at last they faced the Horrible Darkness. FLASH! Fur changed into her heroic form and they took to the sky. The Horrible Darkness thought nothing could stop it, so it dared to face them alone. 'I am Sir Flynnian of Twist World, champion of the Five Islands, and this is the mighty steed, Crystal Fur,' cried Sir Flynnian. 'Behold the Burp of Light!'" Flynn pressed his fists to his hips and went on. "At Sir Flynnian's command, Crystal Fur unleashed her power – *the Burp of Light* – and the Horrible Darkness was destroyed! Light returned to Twist World. The Five Islands were free and Sir Flynnian and Crystal Fur were given medals by all the Islands except the Island of Cheese, who gave them some cheese. They ate the cheese and then off they went on their next brave quest. The End."

Flynn looked back at Fur, hoping that his story had jogged her memory. The dragon was curled up, fast asleep. Flynn's sigh was long and resigned. Perhaps she would never change. Perhaps now she was real, Fur was just plain Fur.

The thought shook him back to reality. He'd unimagined Fur when he needed her most – she'd appeared to protect his sister from the Nobody. Now Nellie was at home with his gran and, quite possibly, the very person who had unimagined the Nobody in the first place – the boy over the road. Flynn felt a sudden pang of guilt in the pit of his stomach.

"I should go home," he said to himself. He poked his head out of the bus shelter. The sun was now a crimson haze on the horizon and the moon had taken its place in the sky.

Flynn rubbed the top of Fur's head to wake her. Then he zipped his coat all the way to the top and grabbed his backpack.

"Come on," he said. "It's getting dark."

Flynn and Fur took the long way back to avoid
going near the windmill, so by the time they
reached the allotments at the edge of the village,
darkness had well and truly fallen. The moon
glowed behind gathering clouds, its bluish
light picking out the shape of Doug Dringle,
standing on his plot. Flynn did a double take. It
wasn't that he was still there – Doug
Dringle was *always* there – but he
wasn't moving. Not an inch. He
was standing there, as still as a
statue.

Flynn squinted in the
darkness and realized
Doug Dringle was
staring right back at him.
Then:

## FPPPPT.

Doug Dringle's fart rang out through the night sky.

Flynn and Fur picked up their pace.

The pair made their way past the church and kept going until they reached the tiny village green. It was darker than ever.

"You OK, Fur?" Flynn whispered to his friend. "I'm OK..."

He couldn't have sounded less convinced. Flynn had never been scared of the dark before but since seeing the Nobody, it seemed like he was scared of *everything*.

As they passed the old oak tree, tiny dots of light flickered in the branches. Flynn gave them a nervous sideways glance. After a moment he realized that they weren't lights at all.

They were crows' eyes.

Dozens of bright white beads reflected in

the moonlight, staring down at them in still silence.

"Fur...?" Flynn whispered. The dragon stayed close to his heels, her tiny ears pinned back, the hairs on her back standing up.

Flynn sped up to a trying-not-to-look-like-you're-running run as he hurried past the village shop. He didn't even see Mrs McCoffey standing in the window with the lights off, staring blankly, as still and silent as a freeze frame.

By the time he and Fur turned into their road, Flynn was breathless. He spotted his gran's house, and then something else – next door's gate, creaking loosely on its hinges.

Suddenly, Fur started to growl, low and steady. Flynn looked ahead to see a large shape in the middle of the road. A gasp caught in his throat.

It was next door's dog.

Rocky Two was loose.

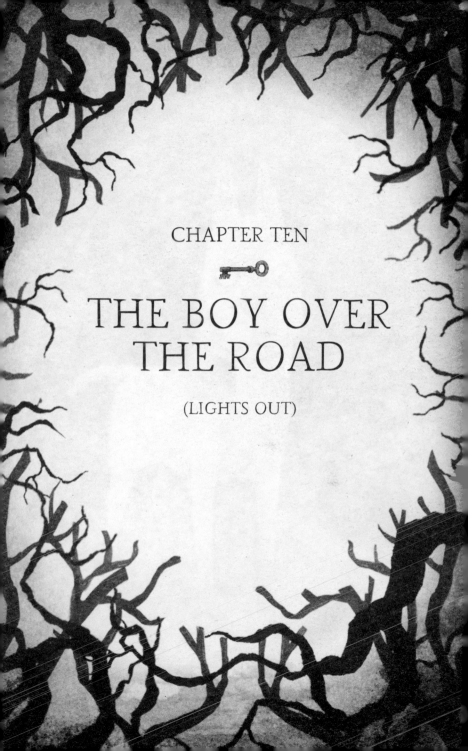

CHAPTER TEN

# THE BOY OVER THE ROAD

(LIGHTS OUT)

*"As dogs love bones, so I do not love dogs."*
—SK

"Oh *no*..." whispered Flynn as the dog loomed there in the moonlight. It looked even bigger without a fence in front of it. Flynn was ready to run but he knew he couldn't outrun a dog.

Suddenly, Fur stopped growling and Flynn realized the dog wasn't barking. In fact, it was making no sound at all.

*Is it getting ready to attack?* thought Flynn. *Or is it—*

FPPT.

The dog's fart was deep and echoing.

The sound of wet thunder.

Flynn's jaw fell open. First Old Mr Nash, then Doug Dringle, now Rocky Two. All the same – all still, all staring, all farting. What was going on? Even the birds stopped and stared at him. Could birds fart? Flynn had no idea. Either way, they all seemed to be acting in the same strange, detached way. Could the Nobody have got to them all already? Memories of Old Mr Nash came without warning. Standing in the windmill in the dark.

"'When darkness falls'," Flynn whispered. "'The Nobody will be here ... there ... everywhere.'"

He looked over the dog's head to his gran's house. If he was going to get there, he had to get past Rocky Two. He picked up Fur and then, despite himself, took a step forwards. He tried to imagine he was brave Sir Flynnian but his legs trembled with every step. The dog did not move. Another step. Then another. Flynn glanced down at Fur, tense and hunched in his arms. Then he looked back at the dog.

Rocky Two was looking straight at him. Flynn froze. The dog's jaw fell open and its long tongue lolled out. A moment later, thick, black shadows began to billow from its mouth.

Flynn ran.

He raced past the dog as fast as he could and hurried to his front door. Cradling Fur in one arm, he reached into his pocket. His hands were trembling as he took out his keys and fumbled for the lock.

"Don't go in there," said a voice.

Flynn spun round, his key hovering by the lock. The boy over the road was right behind him. Flynn felt Fur's breath against his face as she looked up at him, but she didn't make a sound.

"How much
do you know?"
the boy said.
"How much
do you know
about me?"

*I know you unimagined the Nobody,* Flynn thought. His key scratched at the lock as he peered up the street to see if the dog was following him.

"Did your gran tell you about me?" the boy asked.

"W-what?" Flynn said.

"Never mind, it'll take too long," said the boy. Then he quickly added, "I saw the shadow thing coming out of your window last night. I tried to warn your gran but she wouldn't listen. She thought if we stirred up trouble, the *skeleton* would come after us. But something's happening in Matching Trousers ... I think your gran's in danger."

"Danger?" Flynn repeated, his blood running cold. Finally, his key slid into the lock.

"Don't go inside," said the boy, pointing at the front window. "The lights..."

Flynn looked. It was pitch-dark inside the

house. The lights were off.

"Oh *no*," Flynn whispered. "Gran ... Nellie!"

He turned the key in the lock and pushed open the door. He heard the boy shout, "Wait—" as he raced into the house. He slammed the door behind him and bolted it from inside.

"Gran...?" he whispered. Fur leaped to the floor and started sniffing about as Flynn reached for the light switch. His fingers scraped along the wall.

Then, in the light-swallowing darkness, came a sound he had started to dread.

# FFPPT.

# CHAPTER ELEVEN

# TROUBLE AT HOME

## (GOT)

*"Ol' Mr Keys never fails! But just in case,*
*there is Daisy."*
—SK

At the sound of the fart, Flynn's hand found the light switch. Fur yapped as light flooded the room.

"Aaah!" screamed Flynn's gran, waking up with a start.

"AAAH!" shrieked Flynn. He blinked in the brightness. His gran was in her chair. She wafted the air around her knees.

"Don't judge me," she said. "When you get to my age, farts come when they please."

"What's happened? What's going on? Are you OK? Why were the lights off?" gabbled

Flynn in a single, urgent breath.

"Who naps with the lights on?" said Gran. "Everything's *fine*, Flynn. What's with all the questions?"

Flynn breathed a sigh of relief that took all the strength out of him. He fell back against the door and slumped on to the mat.

"Wait, where's Nellie?" he asked.

"Upstairs, sleeping like a proverbial baby, for once," Gran replied, giving a grateful Fur a stroke. "So, how was your day of adventuring, Sir Flynnian? Did you complete your quest and deliver who-knows-what to you-know-who?"

Flynn looked his gran straight in the eye, a shiver running up and down his spine. "Gran, something's happened to Old Mr Nash," he said.

"Happened?" repeated Gran. "He didn't shave his moustache, did he? I can't be doing with a bald top lip..."

Flynn took a deep breath. "So, that shadow in Nellie's room is called the Nobody and it took over Old Mr Nash and it wants to take over everybody and the boy over the road – is he your friend? – I think he unimagined the Nobody and Skeleton Keys said it was a Shady Character so it's not imaginary and it's not real and it wants to find a body of its own and I think it got Doug Dringle too and the crows and Rocky Two and—"

"*Stop*," said Gran. "You need to say words in an order that makes sense to an old woman, Flynn. What's all this gibberish? What's a 'nobody'? And did you say you've had another run-in with Mr Keys?"

Flynn looked back at the door, wondering whether the boy over the road was still outside. He took a deep breath.

"So, it all started when—"

Nellie's wail was loud and startled. Flynn gasped.

## "Nellie? Nellie!"

"Flynn...?" began his gran but a panicking Flynn was already halfway up the stairs. He didn't even imagine what might be waiting for him – all he felt was desperate, clawing fear – but with Fur on his heels, he raced breathlessly up on to the landing and pushed open the door to his sister's bedroom.

"Hello, Run-a-Wayne."

It was Daisy. As she clambered awkwardly through the open window, Nellie blubbed unhappily at the sight of the invader.

"What are you doing here? Where's Mr Keys? Why are you climbing through the—?" Flynn began, but Daisy craned an arm behind her and lifted a finger to her lips.

"*Shh*," she whispered. "You're in trouble."

"W-what?" Flynn said, rushing over to the

crying Nellie and hoisting her out of her cot. "What do you mean?"

"I mean, he got *got*."

"He got got? Who got got?"

"Bone-bag," Daisy said after a pause. "The Nobody got bone-bag."

"Mr Keys?" Flynn gasped. "H-how? What happened?"

"What do you think happened, you soggy bog roll?" Daisy replied. "We went to the windmill to sort out your mess. Bone-bag went in all bones blazing, as usual. An old man with a silly moustache was there. He called himself the Nobody and he said he wanted everybody to be the Nobody."

"Old Mr Nash! See, I told you!" Flynn said. "What did you do?"

"I scared him out of his socks, obviously," Daisy replied matter-of-factly. "He didn't even put up a fight."

"Wait, you got him?"

"I didn't say that," Daisy huffed. "I *knew* it was a trap because I'm good at trap-spotting ... but the bone-headed bone-bag thought the old man was giving up. He didn't even see the fish."

"Fiss!" declared Nellie.

"The *fish*? Like, in the fishbowl?"

"Obviously," said Daisy with a tut. "The Nobody had got the fish too. While bone-bag kept his eye-socket on the old man, the fish zapped him some shady stuff. He got him ... the Nobody *got* him."

"Oh no," Flynn said, queasy with fear. "How did you get away?"

"I went invisible – it's not running away when you're invisible," Daisy replied defensively. "And I didn't walk miles so you could stand here asking stupid questions. *You* unimagined this mess ... now you need to fix it."

"I already told you, I didn't do this!" Flynn said in an urgent whisper. "I didn't unimagine the Nobody – I think it was the boy over the road!"

Daisy ground her teeth so loudly Flynn could hear it. "This isn't the trouble I was

after … I wanted to see a beast. Now bone-
bag's gone," she muttered. She looked away,
and at last Flynn saw a flash of desperation in
Daisy's wild eyes.

"I'm sorry," said Flynn.

"Shut up," Daisy said. "Don't you dare feel
sorry for me, you—"

CLICK
CLUNK

Daisy froze.

"What?"

"Shh." Daisy tilted her head to one side.
Fur tilted her own head the other way as her
antennae twitched.

"What is it?" Flynn whispered.

Daisy's eyes narrowed.

"He's here."

"Who?"

"Who do you think?" Daisy tutted. "Time
to go. Out of the window, Peter Pant-wetter."

"Wait, Mr Keys? Are you saying Mr Keys is *here*?" whispered Flynn, glancing back to the doorway. "Gran!"

"Don't you *dare* go down there," Daisy snapped. But Flynn did not pause. With his sister cradled in his arms, he turned and sped out of the room.

Nobody is here.

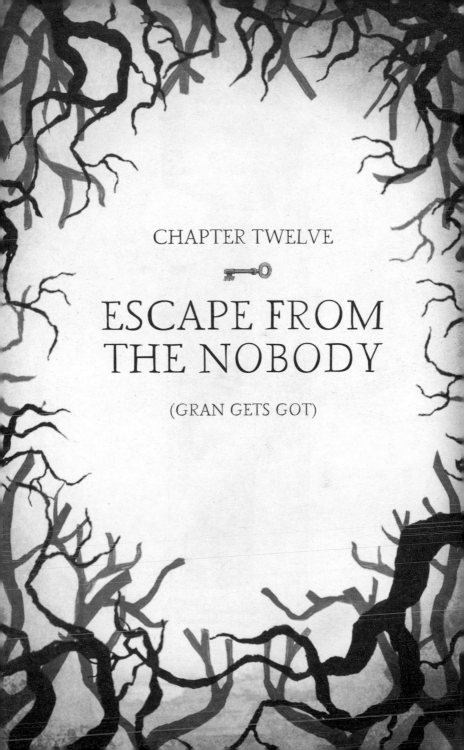

CHAPTER TWELVE

ESCAPE FROM
THE NOBODY

(GRAN GETS GOT)

*The Nobody is here ... there ... everywhere.*

"Gran!"

Flynn's gran was still in her chair when Flynn leaped down the last three stairs into the living room. The door of the grandfather clock was already open as Skeleton Keys clambered out from inside.

"Gran, *run!*" Flynn cried as Fur joined him at his heels.

Gran turned to see the skeleton looming over her.

"Mr Keys?" she said. "I thought I told you not to—"

"Skeleton Keys isn't here," said the skeleton, his voice eerily flat and emotionless. "The Nobody is here."

In an instant, dense, dark shadows began to billow from the skeleton's open mouth. They engulfed Gran's head entirely, swirling round her, until she let out a desperate gasp. The shadows flowed into her open mouth and disappeared.

Flynn's gran froze, her eyes squeezed shut.

"G-Gran...?" Flynn whispered. He saw his gran's eyes slowly open.

"Gran isn't here," she said, rising from her chair. Her voice was cold and detached. "The Nobody is here ... there ... everywhere. Soon, the Nobody will be everybody and—"

*FPPPT.*

Gran's fart stopped her in her tracks.

"—And everybody will be the Nobody," she continued.

"No'dy!" cried Nellie, oblivious to the danger.

"Everybody *must* be the Nobody," added Skeleton Keys, closing in on Flynn as he backed away towards the door.

"D-don't...!" pleaded Flynn, hugging Nellie to him. By now, he was pressed against the door and Fur was all but wound around his ankles.

"First Matching Trousers ... then the world," said Gran as shadows began to puff out of her mouth. "There's no escape. Everybody must be—"

"*Oi*," said a voice. Skeleton Keys and Flynn's gran glanced up the stairs. On the landing stood Daisy, pushing Nellie's cot to the top step. As it tottered there, Daisy added, "It's *nap* time, you Nobodies."

With a final shove, she sent the cot tumbling down the stairs. It crashed into the skeleton, sending him stumbling backwards into Flynn's gran – and the pair crumpled to the floor in a heap.

"Run," said Daisy, hurrying awkwardly downstairs. "Run!"

Flynn pulled open the door and raced outside with Nellie clutched to him. Fur waited until Daisy had made it out of the door and then scurried along behind her. Skeleton Keys was already back on his feet by the time Daisy slammed the door shut.

"What do we do?" Flynn howled in desperation. "Where do we go?"

"Away," replied Daisy. "You *like* running away, Run-a-Wayne, so you shouldn't have any—"

"Daisy, *look*," Flynn interrupted, peering in horror up the street. Next door's dog was still

there, silent and still and staring into the dark
– but then came the neighbours.

They saw one ... two ... a dozen or so
more. Every last one of his gran's neighbours
stepped out of their houses in silent unison.
They slowly made their way into the street
and, all at once, turned to face him. The
air was still. Only the sound of the odd fart
echoed eerily down the street.

"It – it got them," whispered Flynn, dread
gripping him as tightly as he held his sister.
"The Nobody got the neighbours."

"The Nobody told you, there is no escape,"
said a voice from behind them. Flynn spun
round to see Skeleton Keys step out of the
front door with his gran following behind.

"Nobody ahead ... Nobody behind ...
nowhere to run," said Gran. She was right.
Both ends of the street were blocked.

Daisy shrugged. "Well, I tried," she said.

"I'm going to turn invisible now. Good luck
not getting turned into a total Nobody."

"What? You can't!" cried Flynn as the
neighbours began closing in, with Rocky Two
leading the slow advance.

"Can too," Daisy replied. "I'm not your crybaby sitter – you're on your own."

"No, he's not," said a small, thin voice. Flynn looked round to see the boy over the road crossing the street and heading straight for them.

"Oh no – *that's him*," Flynn whispered.

"Who?" Daisy asked.

"The boy over the road," replied Flynn. "He's the one who unimagined the Nobody!"

"That weasel-face?" scoffed Daisy.

"Get behind me," the boy insisted, putting himself between them and the advancing neighbours.

"Flynn-ochio here says you unimagined the Nobody, *Weasel Gummidge*," said Daisy, tapping the boy over the road on the shoulder. "Is he lying again?"

"Far be it from me to accuse anyone of lying," replied the boy. "But I didn't unimagine anyone. Unimaginaries can't unimagine – everybody knows that."

"What?" gasped Flynn. "*You're* unimaginary?"

"Didn't your gran tell you? I'm her IF," said the boy, a smile flashing across his face as he squared up to the advancing villagers.

"I'm the Beast of Matching Trousers."

And, with that, the boy began to *change*.

CHAPTER THIRTEEN

# THE BEAST OF MATCHING TROUSERS

(SOME RESCUE)

*You will be the Nobody too.*

In a blur of movement, the boy over the road transformed. Suddenly he was twice as big as next door's dog. A second later he toppled forwards on to his hands, which were suddenly no longer hands but clawed paws. The boy's body elongated impossibly as his head sprouted pointed ears and a long snout. In moments, he had become a hunched, wolf-like creature, muscular, hairless and tar-black, with gnashing teeth and glowing, ice-white eyes.

A *beast*.

"About time," said Daisy with a lopsided grin. Fur yapped happily at the beast, but Flynn peered up in wide-eyed horror.

"B-Beast of Matching Trousers..." he stuttered. The beast fixed its burning white eyes upon him ... then wheeled round to face the neighbours.

## "LEAVE. THEM. ALONE."

The beast's voice was a bone-shaking roar. The possessed villagers stopped in their tracks, halting their slow and sinister advance.

## "GET BACK," the beast thundered.

# "BACK, OR I'LL EAT YOU ALIVE!"

The beast's voice echoed through the air. Then there was only the eerie wind and the occasional fart. Flynn was sure they were going to run away in horror. After all, that was what he wanted to do.

From behind him, Skeleton Keys broke the silence.

"You will be the Nobody too," he said. "*Everybody* will be the Nobody."

With that, the villagers continued their slow, flatulent advance, unfazed by the beast's threats.

"Can't say we didn't warn them," said Daisy. "Right, beast, get on with it. Just don't swallow bone-bag's keys, I need them." The beast let out another growl and dug its claws into the ground, its long ears pressed against the side of its head. Then it took a step back. "What are you waiting for?" Daisy added impatiently. "*Eat* them."

The beast spun round to face her.

"THERE IS NO WAY I'M ACTUALLY GOING TO EAT PEOPLE," it said, in a whisper as loud as a road drill.

"Why not?" Daisy asked.

"BECAUSE IT'S PEOPLE!" replied the beast. "I DON'T EVEN EAT *DAIRY*. I JUST – I THOUGHT I COULD SCARE THEM OFF..."

"Ugh, some rescue," Daisy groaned, reaching her hand around her back and slapping her palm against her forehead. "Silly softy beasty ... why can't monsters just be monsters?"

The neighbours' farts grew louder as they closed in. By now, they were only a few paces away. Dark clouds of shadow began to billow from their open mouths. The beast let out a sudden, frustrated grunt and crouched low.

**"THIS IS GETTING OUT OF HAND,"** it boomed. Its great head swung towards Flynn and Daisy. **"GET ON MY BACK. HURRY!"**

Fur wasted no time in leaping up on to the beast's back. That was all the prompting Flynn needed. He unzipped his coat halfway and shoved Nellie inside, then zipped it back up, holding her fast, and clambered up on to the beast.

"I'm not climbing on you," Daisy tutted. "You're all monstery."

**"THEN STAY HERE ... AND BE NOBODY,"** snarled the beast. Daisy looked back at Skeleton Keys and saw shadows rising in plumes from inside his skull.

"Ugh, *fine*," she moaned. "But I get to ride up front."

CHAPTER FOURTEEN

# RETURN TO THE WINDMILL

(A PLACE TO HIDE)

*Soon, everybody will be the Nobody.*

Flynn had barely grabbed Daisy's arm
before the beast spun round to face
Skeleton Keys and Flynn's gran. He felt his
stomach lurch as the beast leaped into the air
and straight over Skeleton Keys' head.

"Wait!" cried the skeleton.

Flynn held on for dear life, his sister pressed
between his chest and the beast's back, Fur
curled under his arm, and Daisy's backside
shoved in his face.

"Stop the bus, I want to get off," huffed
Daisy as the Beast of Matching Trousers

conveyed her, Flynn, Nellie and Fur through the village.

"STOP?" panted the beast. "WHY?"

"Because I don't want to spend another second with Flynn-ochio, that's why," Daisy replied. Since her head was on back to front, she managed to glare at Flynn even though he was behind her. "Tried to blame the Nobody on beasty-boy, didn't you, Flynn-ochio? But it was *you* all along."

"It wasn't!" Flynn protested.

"Was too!"

"Was not!"

"IF YOU DON'T STOP ARGUING BACK THERE, I'M GOING TO TURN AROUND AND DELIVER YOU *BOTH* TO THE NOBODY," growled the beast.

"He started it," Daisy huffed.

"Did not!" said Flynn.

"Did too!"

"ENOUGH!" the beast boomed.
"I CAN'T RUN FOREVER. INSTEAD
OF SQUABBLING, WHY DON'T YOU
PUT YOUR HEADS TOGETHER AND
TRY TO THINK OF A PLACE FOR US
TO HIDE OUT."

Flynn and Daisy scowled at each other but the same thought occurred to them. Though neither of them was keen to return, neither of them could think of a better place to hide, so the same word escaped their lips.

"*Windmill.*"

The Beast of Matching Trousers took the long way round to the windmill, so as to avoid the village. It slumped to the ground in exhaustion when they reached the top of Trouser Hill. The white tower loomed in the moonlight.

"The lights are still off –
do you think Old Mr
Nobody Nash is still in there?"
whispered Flynn as he climbed
down from the beast's back.
He checked on Nellie,
who somehow had
fallen asleep. Fur
leaped on to his back
and curled round
his shoulders as he crept
towards the door.

"All I know is, last time we let ourselves in, the old bone-bag got *got* – this time we do it the Daisy Way," said Daisy, clambering awkwardly off the beast's back. She made her way to the door. "Beasty-boy, make sure you eat the old man as soon as he comes out."

"JUST HURRY UP," said the beast.

Daisy grinned and rang the bell twice. She immediately turned invisible. Flynn panicked and pressed himself against the wall next to the door.

There was silence, a bubbling parp of a fart and the creak of a turning handle. No sooner had Old Mr Nash stepped out on to his own welcome mat, cradling his fishbowl, than the beast grabbed the collar of his shirt in its powerful jaws. With a flick of its great head, it sent both man and fishbowl rolling down the hill. Daisy reappeared with a disappointed huff.

"Are you not going to eat anyone *at all*?" she moaned.

"WOULD YOU GET INSIDE?" snarled the beast.

Flynn made his way through the door with Daisy close behind. He heard the beast try to squeeze through the doorway, its great shoulders jammed against the sides of the door frame.

"BOTHER, I'M STUCK," it growled. In a haze of movement, it shifted and shrank until, in a few short seconds, the Beast of Matching Trousers had been replaced by the boy over the road. He hurried inside, slammed the door behind him and bolted it. "Home, sweet hideout," he said. "Leave the lights off so they don't know we're here."

"Do you think we'll be safe?" Flynn asked as Fur sniffed the air from atop his shoulders.

"Bone-bag can unlock any door, or make

doors where there aren't any, so *no*," replied Daisy. "I knew this was a silly plan."

"Then why didn't you say so?" Flynn said as Fur yapped at Daisy. "You said we should come to the windmill just like I—"

"Would you two please pack it in?" interrupted the boy. "We need to stick together or we'll be possessed by the Nobody before the night is over."

"And whose fault is that?" said Daisy.

"For the last time, I didn't unimagine the Nobody!" shouted Flynn.

"Then who did?" Daisy began.

"I don't—"

"STOP it, the pair of you," the boy yelled, just a hint of beastliness in his voice. After a moment's silence he rubbed his eyes. "Look, just get some rest. I have a feeling it's going to be a long night."

"It's been too long already," moaned Daisy.

Even in the dark Flynn could feel Daisy's burning glower. He wished he'd never had the misfortune to run into her. But he had to admit, her question was a good one.

If the boy over the road didn't unimagine the Nobody, who did?

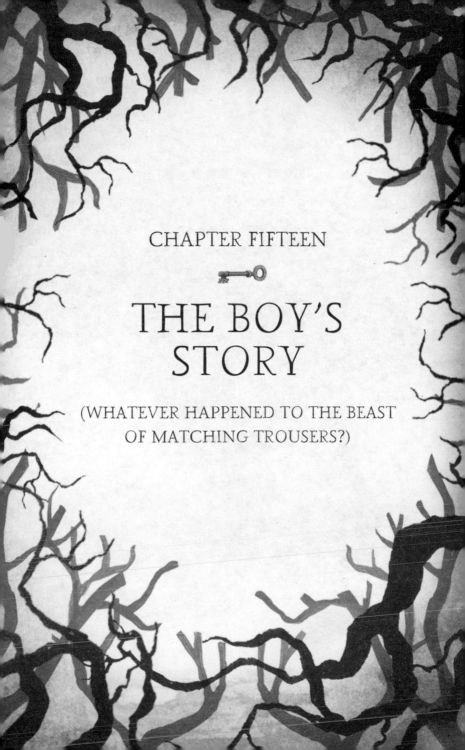

# CHAPTER FIFTEEN

# THE BOY'S STORY

### (WHATEVER HAPPENED TO THE BEAST OF MATCHING TROUSERS?)

*There is no escape from the Nobody.*

O nly fear kept Flynn awake. He wasn't
sure how many hours had passed in the
darkness. He, Daisy and the boy over the road
sat in a circle on the floor of the windmill.

As his sister snored in his arms and Fur
napped on his crossed legs, Flynn felt heavy
and sluggish with exhaustion – but cold
panic kept his eyes from closing. He glanced
at Daisy, whose head lolled to one side as
she slept, then at the boy, not quite able to
believe he was once too big and beastly to
fit through the front door.

"Can't sleep?" said the boy over the road in a whisper. Flynn realized he was looking straight at him.

"I – I wasn't staring," said Flynn quickly.

"Were too," said the boy with a smile. "Was it because I'm a beast, or do you still think I unimagined the Nobody?"

Flynn blushed. "Sorry," he whispered. "I thought it had to be you."

"You can be forgiven a stretch of the imagination," said the boy. He gestured towards Fur. "After all, a wild imagination runs in the family."

"This is her normal form. Her heroic form is— Never mind," Flynn said with a sigh. "When did Gran unimagine you?"

"She was just a bit younger than you," the boy replied. "I didn't look like this then – your gran unimagined the beast, and let me tell you, I *liked* being a beast. I was big and strong and I had excellent teeth. It didn't occur to either of us that my appearance might upset the locals – but before we knew it everyone was screaming and panicking and running about. They thought I was dangerous and ran away or hid whenever I appeared. To be honest, I quite enjoyed being frightening. We were left to do what we wanted! That is, until the skeleton came. He thought I was *dangerous* ... and the townsfolk were inclined to agree. In no time, they wanted to be free of the Beast of Matching Trousers, so the skeleton tried to get rid of me. I don't know what he had planned for me but I wasn't about to find out. Fortunately, your gran imagined me with a gift – she imagined I could become *human*."

"Is that when you changed?" said Flynn.

The boy looked down at his hands.

"No one saw me change but your gran.

The skeleton was none the wiser – as far as he was concerned, the beast had vanished off the face of the earth. In the end, he gave up looking. I was left to grow up – but I did not age. I still looked like a child when your gran was having children of her own. I started to feel like I was getting in the way ... or perhaps I was just jealous that I was no longer the most important person in her life. Your gran was kind enough to buy me the house over the road so I could still be close to her, but it was never quite the same for either of us. It's not easy being unimaginary. People change ... but we change too."

Flynn glanced wistfully down at Fur.

"Or don't," he said.

"Your gran said Fur doesn't remember who she really is," said the boy. "Perhaps she's waiting for you to remember who *you* are."

"What do you mean?"

"Sir Flynnian of Twist World, isn't it?" whispered the boy. "Champion of the Five Islands?"

"That's just … fan fiction."

"Maybe, or maybe you just need the right motivation. After all, I vowed never again to become the beast, but I had no choice."

A tear welled in Flynn's eye and he quickly wiped it away.

"It's my fault – I should have stopped Mr Keys from getting Gran," he said.

"I'm as much to blame," said the boy. "I knew something was wrong but I waited too long to act. And we still don't even know where the Nobody came from."

"*Do too*," hissed Daisy. Flynn glanced over to see her awake and eyeballing him again. "I had Flynn-ochio pegged from the start."

"That's enough, young lady," said the boy firmly. "We can't afford not to trust each other. Fear makes people suspicious ... it makes them look for someone to blame."

"You'd better not be calling me a scaredy-coward, beasty-boy," Daisy snarled.

"The point is, the Nobody is a true monster," the boy said. "I mean, I'm an actual beast, and I've never encountered such menace. Do you really believe Flynn could imagine something so *horrible*?"

"I was imagined," said Daisy. "And I'm one hundred per cent horrible."

"H-horrible...?" Flynn mouthed. The word stuck in his throat, and a sudden, terrible thought occurred to him. He remembered the story he had made up for his little sister on the night the Nobody first appeared:

*The Horrible Darkness spread across Twist World. It got everybody. It took them over, until nobody was left.*

It suddenly made a terrifying sort of sense.

How could he not have made the connection sooner? It seemed impossible and obvious at the same time:

The Horrible Darkness *was* the Nobody.

"Oh *no*," Flynn muttered, the words escaping before he could stop them.

"Flynn? Are you all right?" the boy said, seeing the colour drain from Flynn's cheeks. Flynn held his hand to his mouth as tears began to well in his eyes.

"The Horrible Darkness," he whispered, his blood running cold. "It got everybody ... until nobody was left."

"Horrible darkness?" repeated the boy.

"It – it was just a story to help Nellie sleep," Flynn began. "But the Horrible Darkness ... it's just like the Nobody."

"*Wait a minute*," said Daisy, her eyes wild and twitching. "What are you saying? Are you saying you *did* unimagine the Nobody?"

Flynn stared down at his sister, his breath panting and panicked. "I don't know," he said, choking back tears. "Maybe."

"Argh! I knew it, I *knew* it!" Daisy roared. "You stupid, Flynn-ochio, Peter Pant-wetter, Run-a-Wayne! Look what you've done! What am I supposed to do now? What am I supposed to do without the stupid old bone-bag?"

"I'm sorry!" Flynn sobbed. "I didn't know I could unimagine! I didn't even know what unimagining was!"

"Well, now the Nobody's going to take over *everybody* because of your silly, stupid story – and it'll serve you right," Daisy growled.

"Your crusty old gran is going to spend the rest of her life as a brain-drained farty-bum-skunk and it's all your fault!"

"Shut up!" Flynn cried. "You shut up about my—"

FPPT.

At the sound of the fart, everyone froze. Their eyes darted around the darkness.

"... Where did it come from?" the boy whispered.

"*Inside*," Flynn uttered in horror. "It came from—"

FFPPT.

Flynn sniffed the air, winced and slowly looked down. His sister had farted herself awake. She grinned as she peered up at her brother.

"Nellie!" Flynn cried with a leg-trembling sigh of relief as his sister giggled. "You stinky trumpet!"

"Tum-pit!" Nellie giggled.

Flynn couldn't help but laugh.

The boy laughed too then.

Daisy just tutted and rolled her eyes but the laughter was still loud enough to drown out the sounds coming from *outside* the windmill.

FPPT. FP-PT.

PPT.

FPPT.

FFFFPT.

It wasn't until Fur started to growl at the door that Flynn realized something was wrong. He swallowed his laughter in an instant and craned his head to listen.

Farts. Dozens of farts.

The boy was still chuckling as Flynn carried his sister over to the window and peered out. The cool moonlight illuminated numerous figures on the hill. One after the other they came, slowly, flatulently making their way towards the windmill.

It was the villagers.

All three hundred and forty-three of them.

CHAPTER SIXTEEN

# RETURN OF THE BEAST

(RUN)

*In the end, everybody must be the Nobody.*

"Oh *no*," Flynn whispered. "They found us!"

Daisy and the boy over the road hurried to the window and peered out. The villagers were gathering. They were all there – Old Mr Nash, Mrs McCoffey, Doug Dringle – even next door's dog.

"I *said* you should have eaten Old Mr 'Tache," complained Daisy. "They knew where we were the minute we got here."

"How many are out there?" asked the boy.

"I think ... *everybody*," whispered Flynn

as Nellie burbled and squeezed his chin. Then he spotted a familiar figure among the approaching crowd.

"Gran...!" he cried.

"Is bone-bag there?" Daisy asked, craning to look out of the window.

"I – I can't see him," said Flynn. Then he added hopefully, "Maybe he got *un*-got... Maybe he's free and going to rescue us."

"Don't hold your breath, scaredy-coward," said Daisy, secretly hoping that was exactly what had happened.

"Well, we can't sit around waiting to find out," said the boy. He hurried across the room to a window on the opposite wall and peered out. "Maybe we can sneak out the back and make a break for the woods..."

"Run away, *again*?" said Daisy. She growled at Flynn. "Well, the least you could do is give us a head start, Flynn-ochio – go on, get out there and get got."

"I'm not going out there!" Flynn protested.

"Peter Pant-wetter," Daisy sneered.

"They'll turn me into a mindless—"

"Run-a-Wayne."

"I'm not leaving Nellie alone with—"

"Scaredy-coward!"

"Fine! Yes, I'm scared!" Flynn shouted. "I'm a Peter Pant-wetter, Run-a-Wayne, scaredy-coward! You know it and Fur knows it and everyone knows it!"

"Finally we agree on something," said Daisy.

"Stop! I can't hear myself think with you two at each other!" the boy cried, turning away from the window. Between the argument and Fur yapping angrily at Daisy, he didn't even hear the CLICK CLUNK of a key turning in a lock. Nor did he see the door suddenly materialize in the wall behind him ... or the door slide silently open

... or the skeleton step nimbly through the doorway. "I've had it up to here with you! Don't make me tell ... you ... again..."

At the sound of the rattle of bones, the boy trailed off and turned.

"Bother," he whimpered. "Everybody, run!"

Flynn and Daisy spun round to see Skeleton  Keys looming over the boy over the road. A cloud of shadows swirled out of the skeleton's skull and around the boy's head. Then, with a gasp, the boy's mouth fell open and the shadows disappeared down his throat.

"... Bone-bag?" whispered Daisy, her faint hope that Skeleton Keys had escaped the Nobody's influence immediately dissolving.

"That's better," said the skeleton.

"Yes," said the boy, his voice flat and cold. "The Nobody is here."

The boy had already started to change shape when Daisy told Flynn to run. Flynn clutched his sister to him as Daisy grabbed his arm and pulled him towards the front door. By the time she'd reached for the door handle, the boy over the road had once again become the Beast of Matching Trousers.

"*Run!*" Daisy yelled again.

# "THERE IS NO ESCAPE FROM THE NOBODY,"

the beast boomed. Flynn glanced back to see it hurtle across the room towards them.

Daisy had barely managed to pull open the door as the beast's shadow fell over them. Flynn leaped through the doorway after her, carrying Nellie in his arms. He heard the snap of the beast's jaws as he tripped over Old Mr

Nash's welcome mat. He spun on to his back as he tumbled to the ground, landing with a painful thump. As he sat up, he heard the sound of a high-pitched squeal – and realized that Fur wasn't on his shoulders any more. He looked back at the windmill.

The first thing Flynn saw was the beast, once again trapped in the doorway, teeth gritted, straining against the splintering wood of the door frame. But then he noticed something caught between two of the beast's teeth.

"Fur!" he cried. Sure enough, she was snagged by the tail, dangling helplessly from the beast's mouth. The beast shook its head, left, then right, and Flynn saw Fur fly through the air and land in a limp heap on the ground. He called Fur's name again as he got to his feet, racing over to her and scooping her up in his free arm.

She whimpered, weakly, but did not move.

Flynn held her to
his chest as the
unnumbered
eyes of the
villagers stared
at him – human,
animal – even the crows
from the oak tree looked
down on him as they circled
overhead.

In that moment, Flynn wished more than
anything for the ground to swallow him and
his sister and his unimaginary friend up – to
disappear forever rather than face what was
to come.

Daisy joined Flynn at his side. "I'm going
invisible now," she said. There was a long
pause … but she remained well and truly
visible. Finally, she added a disgruntled,
"Ugh, let's just get this over with."

Flynn's gran said:

"In the end, everybody must be the Nobody."

Three hundred and forty-three voices rang out:

"Everybody must be the Nobody."

"Yeah, you mentioned that," groaned Daisy.

"A *million* times."

"But *why*?" Flynn sobbed. "Please,
I didn't mean to unimagine you! It was just
a story ... you don't have to do this because
of me!"

"You? This has nothing to do with you,"
said his gran. "You did not imagine the
Nobody. She did."

"She...?" Flynn grunted, looking at the girl
with the backwards head. "Wait, *Daisy*?"

"No, not her," said Gran and pointed at
Flynn's sister. "Nellie."

CHAPTER SEVENTEEN

# NIGHT OF THE NOBODY

(NELLIE)

*There must be only the Nobody and Nellie.*

"*Nellie?*" said Flynn with a gasp. "Nellie didn't imagine you, she's just a baby! She doesn't have anything to do with this!"

PPPT.

Flynn's gran casually wafted at her backside.

"Of course she did," she said. "Wild imaginations run in the family."

"Nellie was alone, so she imagined the Nobody for company," said Old Mr Nash, stepping out of the crowd with a moustache full of grass from his tumble down the hill.

He was carrying his fish, which flapped around in the few drops of water left in its bowl. "But Nellie's wild imagination made the Nobody *real*."

"No'dy!" squealed Nellie happily, blissfully unaware of the unfolding horrors. To Flynn, it suddenly felt like the missing part of the puzzle. He had told his sister the story of *Sir Flynnian versus the Horrible Darkness* the night the Nobody appeared in her room. His story had inspired her to create a monster.

"So, basically this is still all your fault, scaredy-coward," Daisy said, as if reading his mind.

"Now everybody must be the Nobody, so Nellie will never be alone," Doug Dringle said flatulently.

"Soon the whole world will be the Nobody," said Mrs McCoffey from the village shop. "There will be only Nellie and the Nobody."

"I am not getting got by a baby's unimaginary friend, it's silly," huffed Daisy.

Then came a roar that echoed over Matching Trousers and beyond, to the neighbouring village of Matching Socks. The windmill's door frame shattered as the Beast of Matching Trousers finally broke free. Flynn spun round to see the beast lumber forwards ... and riding upon its back was Skeleton Keys.

"Bone-bag?" Daisy gasped. The skeleton blankly peered down at her, as if he barely even recognized her. A moment later, the Beast of Matching Trousers reared up dramatically. "Ugh, even when you're possessed, you're a total show-off," Daisy groaned.

"In the end, there must only be Nellie and the Nobody," Skeleton Keys said. The beast paced up and down in front of the villagers and then rounded on Flynn with a long growl

and a short fart. "Nellie belongs with the
Nobody."

"But she *doesn't* belong with you," Flynn
said, tears welling in his eyes. "She belongs
with me. She belongs with her family."

"But soon you will be the Nobody too," said
Skeleton Keys, a cloud of horrible darkness
forming inside his skull.

Flynn looked down at his sister. She gazed back up at him, hungry and confused and possibly wondering why everyone was farting so much. He imagined a world where she would never know anybody because everybody would be the Nobody.

Even her own brother.

Flynn felt that fear, cold and relentless. But something was different – he didn't feel like running away. He placed Fur gently on the ground, then he turned to Daisy and held Nellie out to her with both hands.

"Take her," he said.

"Eww," said Daisy. "I don't want a baby, they smell."

"Please," Flynn said. "Take her and run. Run for the woods. Get her away from them."

For a moment, Daisy looked lost for words.

"What are you going to do?" she said at last.

"I don't know," he said.

"But even if I get away—"

"I know," Flynn interrupted. "*Please*, Daisy."

Daisy shook her head, just a little. But then she turned away so her body faced Flynn and took Nellie in her arms.

"No farting, you," she said as Nellie held out her arms to Flynn with a fearful whimper.

"It's OK, Nell," Flynn said. "Don't be scared."

Then Daisy turned invisible and ran.

# CHAPTER EIGHTEEN

# CRYSTAL FUR

## (NOT RUNNING AWAY)

*Nothing can stop the Nobody.*

Flynn watched Nellie disappear into the darkness. Carried by the invisible Daisy, she looked as if she was floating through the air.

"Why delay the inevitable?" said Skeleton Keys atop the Beast of Matching Trousers, shadows billowing from inside his skull. "We will find her. In the end, there will be only Nellie and the Nobody."

Flynn stroked Fur's limp body as she lay on the grass. Then he took a long, deep breath, got slowly to his feet and faced the skeleton.

"You've got to get past me first," he said, clenching his fists. "And I … am Sir Flynnian of Twist World."

A fart rang out over the hill. A cloud of shadows swirled around Skeleton Keys' skull.

"Not for long," he hissed, the shadows flowing from his skull towards Flynn. "In the end, everybody must be … No … body…"

The skeleton trailed off and Flynn followed his gaze down to his own feet. He suddenly found himself squinting against a shining, white light. It was Fur. The little creature was glowing and growing brighter by the second. Glowing – and *growing*.

Fur grew so quickly that in moments Flynn was looking up at her. She grew and grew until she dwarfed every villager on the hill – bigger, even, than the Beast of Matching Trousers. Then, in a flash of light that made the villagers wail in eerie unison,

Fur was engulfed in a blinding radiance. What emerged in Fur's place was a towering light-dragon formed entirely of shimmering crystal. Moonlight glistened upon her sparkling hide as she reared up and spread a pair of enormous wings, each revealing a hundred crystal feathers, which gleamed with a dazzling excess of bright, shifting colours.

"*Crystal Fur?*" whispered Flynn as the dragon crashed back on to four legs. "You changed ... you *remembered!*"

Crystal Fur beat her wings, lighting up the night sky with colourful flashes. She craned her long neck until she was almost eye to eye with Flynn. He saw his own reflection in the dragon's gleaming face as he reached out to touch her cheek. The light-dragon let out a low, ground-rumbling purr and a rainbow danced across her skin.

"I'm sorry if I made you forget who you are," Flynn said, patting the glittering crystals on the light-dragon's neck. Crystal Fur scooped Flynn up on her snout. He felt himself lifted into the air before sliding swiftly along her head and down her neck, coming to rest between the dragon's shoulders. He spun round and shuffled a little on the light-dragon's back. Rock-hard crystal wasn't quite as comfortable as he'd imagined, but he could not think of a better place than atop his mighty steed.

"You will be the Nobody too!" said Skeleton Keys, a hint of anger at last cracking in his voice as he tried to shield his eyes from the light-dragon's glow. The beast snarled and gnashed its teeth but it too winced against her insistent radiance. At once, Flynn remembered the Nobody shrieking when he switched on the light in Nellie's bedroom.

*The light is its weakness*, Flynn thought. *It fears it, just like the Horrible Darkness ... just like in my story.*

But Flynn knew he did not get to choose how this story ended.

He had to fight for it.

"I think I have a sort of plan, kind of," he whispered to his mighty steed. She beat her wings, illuminating the sky with bursts of light.

"The Nobody is *everybody*," Skeleton Keys howled, and the beast let out a deafening roar.

"Everybody is the Nobody!" echoed the townsfolk in unison.

*The Horrible Darkness thought nothing could stop it,* Flynn thought, recounting the story he'd told his sister, *so it dared to face them alone.*

"No, you're *not* everybody!" yelled Flynn. "You're the Nobody, there's only *one* of you!

Come out and face me!"

"Nothing can stop the Nobody," said the skeleton. "So be it."

In sudden unison, Skeleton Keys and the Beast of Matching Trousers flung their heads back and opened their jaws. Every villager on the hill followed suit as shadows poured out of their mouths in plumes, tendrils of darkness rising upwards. The shadows began to mingle and merge, high above the hill – within seconds they had formed a single, vast creature – the very same creature Flynn had seen in his sister's room the previous night, but a hundred times bigger.

"NO ... BODY," the Nobody roared as it lunged for the light-dragon.

Flynn saw the Nobody's huge, sharp teeth and endless shadows billowing from its mouth.

"Fly, Fur!" Flynn cried. "Fly!"

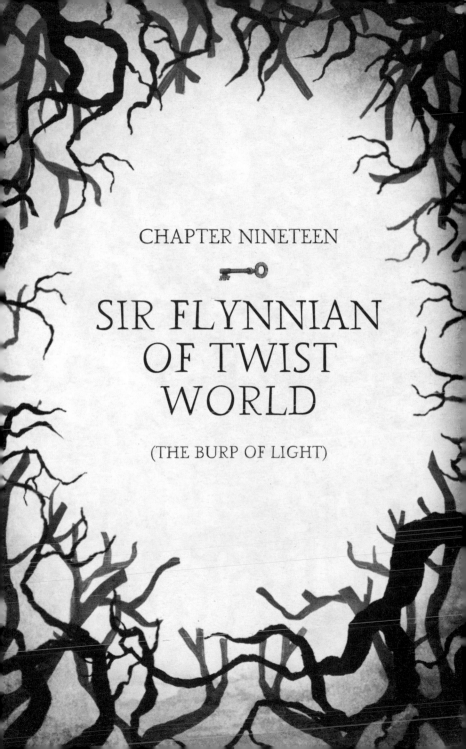

CHAPTER NINETEEN

# SIR FLYNNIAN OF TWIST WORLD

## (THE BURP OF LIGHT)

*"Never underestimate
a wild imagination."*
—SK

"Fur, fly!" Flynn cried again. With a single beat of her shimmering wings, Crystal Fur took to the air. The sound of roaring wind whipped past Flynn's ears with every beat of the light-dragon's wings but it did not drown out the roar of the Nobody itself:

# "NO ... BO ... DY,"

it boomed. As Crystal Fur flew higher, Flynn glanced down to the hundreds of villagers, their mouths flung open, still tethered to the Nobody with dark, shadowy tendrils.

"The Burp of Light!" he cried over

the sound of Crystal
Fur's beating wings. "Use
the Burp of Light, Crystal
F— aAAH!"

A jet of shadows suddenly blasted out
of the Nobody's mouth. Crystal Fur banked
in the air as the jet missed them by an inch.
The Nobody roared, sending another jet
towards the light-dragon. Crystal Fur wheeled
and arced, avoiding blast after blast, circling
around the Nobody and soaring high over its
head. She hovered there, her wings beating
heavily, and Flynn found himself gazing into
the abyss of the Nobody's mouth of shadows.

"I am Sir Flynnian of Twist World," he
whispered, and though he should have felt
more scared than ever, for the briefest of
moments, he felt no fear at all. In fact, it was
everything he'd ever imagined – the hero and
his mighty steed, fighting to save the

world. At the top of his lungs, Flynn cried out:

"I am Sir Flynnian of Twist World, champion of the Five Islands, and this is my mighty steed, Crystal Fur! Behold the Burp of Light!"

Crystal Fur took a deep breath and, with an almighty belch, unleashed a powerful beam of starlight from her gaping jaws. It seared through the shadow. The beam's light seemed to fill the whole sky, bathing the Nobody – and every inch of the hill. For a split second, every tiny suggestion of darkness was driven away.

The Nobody screamed its own name once more and then, with a single, ear-splitting fart, vanished in a flash of brilliance. Even the shadowy tendrils binding it to the villagers disappeared.

In an instant, the banishment was complete. As Crystal Fur's Burp of Light faded, the dazed and dazzled villagers realized where they were – but with no memory of how they got there. Skeleton Keys, meanwhile, was so shocked to find himself riding the Beast of Matching Trousers that he toppled from its back and plummeted to the ground.

"Crumcrinkles!" he said as the beast loomed over him, its teeth bared. "Can it be? The Beast of Matching Trousers! By my buckles, I thought you had vanished off the face of the earth!"

"I NEVER WENT FAR," the beast replied. In an instant he changed again, and where once stood the beast was the boy over the road.

"Dogs 'n' cats, you're the sprout over the road! Why, do not tell me you have been hiding all this time?"

"In plain sight – but not any more," said the boy. "No more hiding."

Then, as the villagers uneasily wondered what they might all be doing on Trouser Hill in the middle of the night, they got a greater shock – a huge dragon formed entirely of crystal, swooping through the air over their heads and coming to a dramatic landing beside the windmill.

"Gran? Gran!" Flynn cried. Crystal Fur lowered her neck to the ground and he slid down it. He hit the ground and raced over to his gran, who was already helping the boy over the road get Skeleton Keys to his feet.

"Flynn!" she said as he ran into her arms. He squeezed her tightly, tears welling in his eyes. "What's going on?" Gran asked. "How did we get here? Where's Nellie?"

"Dogs 'n' cats, my memory is no less soupy 'n' slop about," Skeleton Keys moaned. "Where is Daisy? And why is there a baby floating towards us?"

"A what?" said Gran. Sure enough, a giggling Nellie appeared out of the darkness, apparently hovering towards them through the air.

"Boo," said a voice. A second later, Daisy appeared, holding Nellie at arm's length.

"Nellie!" Flynn cried, racing over to her.

"You could have *told* me not-cat was about to start showing off," Daisy moaned, peering up at Crystal Fur. "You made me do all that stupid running for nothing."

"Sorry about that," said Flynn,

his sigh of relief almost a laugh. "It just sort of happened."

"Well, hurry up and take *this*," Daisy added, jiggling Nellie up and down. "Either I stepped in something or it pooed itself, or both."

"Day-see!" burbled Nellie.

Flynn took Nellie and squeezed her to him. She let out a small but foul-smelling fart.

"Thanks, Daisy," he said, blinking away a tear. "Thank you."

"Yeah, well," said Daisy with a shrug. "*Somebody* had to be a hero."

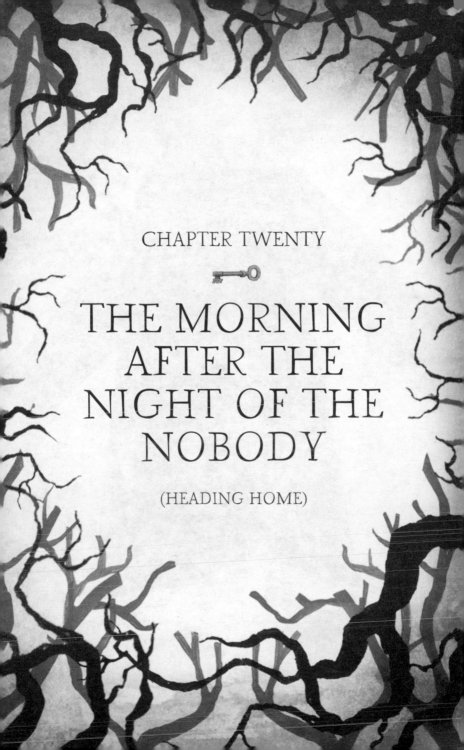

CHAPTER TWENTY

# THE MORNING AFTER THE NIGHT OF THE NOBODY

(HEADING HOME)

*"There is nothing Ol' Mr Keys likes more than a story with a Twist in the tale."*

—SK

Light returned to Matching Trousers. By the time dawn broke over the horizon, even the most bewildered villager had come to their senses and, without exception, felt an overwhelming desire for a good day's sleep. Even the sight of a gleaming light-dragon wasn't enough to keep them from wandering slowly home. Crystal Fur curled up next to the windmill for a nap as Flynn, Nellie, their gran, the boy over the road, Daisy and a puzzled, key-fingered skeleton watched the last of the villagers head home. A warm breeze blew dry orange leaves across the hill.

"Crumcrinkles, I am still having trouble getting my skull around this," confessed Skeleton Keys. "I am as certain as sandwiches that I made my way to the windmill – what happened after that?"

"You messed up again. Luckily, you've got me to save you," said Daisy. She glanced over at Flynn and the others. "Ugh, fine, they helped a *bit* ... but I did all the heavy lifting."

"I would expect nothing less than save-a-day heroism from Sir Flynnian of Twist World!" declared Skeleton Keys, before turning to the boy over the road. "But I admit I misjudged your beastliness, beast. Please accept my sorrowing apology – I treated you most unfairly back in the way-back-when. Despite my years, I am afraid Ol' Mr Keys is still a work in progress."

"Aren't we all," said the boy. "And apology accepted."

"Fine and fantabulant!" declared the skeleton. "Then Daisy and I shall be on our merrisome—"

"Not so fast, Mr Keys," said Gran. "Since it's a day for burying hatchets, you're not going anywhere 'til we've all shared a nice pot of tea. Just once, it'd be nice if you came *invited* into my home."

"Dilys Twist, I could not agree more," said the skeleton.

"Crystal Fur can *fly* us home," Flynn declared proudly, but turned to find that the sleeping light-dragon had once again transformed. The small, drab Fur lay snoring where her heroic form had lain only a moment ago. Flynn smiled and scooped the little dragon up in his arms. "Or we could walk," he added.

By the time they arrived home, everything seemed more or less back to normal, even if the whole village was asleep. One thing had certainly changed though – as Flynn passed by next door's gate, their dog did not bark or attempt to eat him as he expected. In fact, Rocky Two took one look at the little dragon in Flynn's arms and slunk nervously to a corner of the front garden.

"I feel like I could sleep for a week," said the boy over the road as they reached the door to Gran's house. "I may be getting too old for this."

"Sure you won't come in for a cup of tea?" Gran asked.

"Maybe tomorrow," he said with a smile. "After all, I'm never far away."

# CHAPTER TWENTY-ONE

# A GIFT

## (THE GRANDFATHER CLOCK)

*A tale of shadows and of light*
*Of things a-bumping in the night*
*The village found its folk possessed!*
*So heroes rose up to the test*
*For nobody could take from Flynn*
*His world of wild imagining!*

Skeleton Keys and Daisy joined the Twists round the table for breakfast. After watching everyone fill up on much toast and tea, the skeleton offered his second apology of the morning.

"How wretched and regretful I am that you all had to endure such a foulsome and confuddling trial," he began. "I am afraid I let the Nobody treat me like a prize saddle-goose. I should have known better than to be fool-boozled by a Shady Character."

"It's almost as if you're not getting any

better at this," offered Daisy.

"Then it is especially gladdening to have such brave and boldering ankle-sprouts to save the day on my behalf," the skeleton said.

"It was Fur who saved us in the end," Flynn said, stroking the top of her head as she slept. "She remembered who she was just in time."

"So did you, Flynn Gatsinzi Twist – so did you," said Gran. She deposited Nellie in her high chair and kissed her so firmly on the cheek she left a lipstick mark. "And *you*, you little stink bomb! What were you thinking, dreaming up such a nasty piece of work?"

"It's not her fault," said Flynn. "I told her the story of the Horrible Darkness. I gave her the idea for the Nobody."

"No'dy!" shouted Nellie.

"Do not blame yourself, ankle-sprout – a wild imagination is nothing to be ashamed of." He leaned towards Flynn's sister and examined her cautiously. "And – cheese 'n' biscuits! – you Twists seem to have imagination to spare! Though I have never known an unimaginary to spring from the mind of someone so young. I should probably keep a watchful eye socket on this one..."

"Don't worry, we'll do our best to keep our little Twist out of trouble," said Flynn's gran. After a moment, she added, "But you're welcome to pop by any time, Mr Keys. Just try not to bring *quite* so much trouble with you next time."

"No trouble?" Daisy said. "No chance."

Skeleton Keys bowed low to Flynn's gran, and then suddenly looked at his bone wrist as if glancing at a watch.

"Crumcrinkles! Is that the time? We must be away, Daisy! Adventure awaits!" He made his way to the front door in two large strides and swung it open as if to leave … then he paused. He scratched his head with all ten key-tipped fingers and glanced over at the old grandfather clock in the corner of the room. In another long stride he reached it and slid a key-tipped thumb into the lock on the door.

"Before I go, I have a gift for you, 'Sir Flynnian'," said Skeleton Keys, holding out his other hand. Flynn took it and with a CLICK CLUNK, the skeleton pulled open the door. Flynn was once again confronted by the sight of his own imagination. The Five Islands of Earth, Air, Fire, Cheese and Crystal. Twist World, suspended in a sky that went on forever.

"I – I don't understand…" Flynn uttered.

"With the *Key to Imagination*, I have once again created a doorway to the world you created," Skeleton Keys explained. "But this time, I intend to leave the door open."

"Open?" repeated Flynn, looking down at the sleeping Fur.

"I thought perhaps you and your mighty steed might fancy a visit every now and again," said Skeleton Keys. "As long as the door remains open, you may come and go to Twist World as you wish. You and Christoph— *Crystal Fur* may soar the skies above your imagined land as if it were as real as Matching Trousers. Although perhaps you might want to put the grandfather clock somewhere less conspicuous..."

Flynn wasn't entirely sure what happened next, except that he found himself running into Skeleton Keys' arms to give him a hug. The skeleton felt undeniably bony. Still, Flynn held him for a long moment and said, "Thank you, Mr Keys."

"By my buckles, ankle-sprout, it is the very least I could do," replied the skeleton. Flynn at last let him go, then Skeleton Keys swept back to the front door. "To wild imaginations!" he declared as Daisy ambled through.

And with that, he stepped outside and pulled the door shut.

*S*o there we have it, dallywanglers! The truly unbelievable, unbelievably true tale that I have chosen to call *The Night of the Nobody*. Did I not tell you it was a hum-dum-dinger? I have never known a barely sprouted sprout like Nellie Twist to conjure an unimaginary all of their own – though it seems she found inspiration from her brother's flabbergasting fables. A fantabulant family of wild imaginers, indeed!

And I assure you, dallywanglers, I shall never again be fool-boozled into playing the villain. Ask anyone – I really am among the most heroic, good-do-well skeletons you are ever likely to meet...

Well, Ol' Mr Keys' work is never done – I already feel the twitch in my bones. Who knows where it will lead? Perhaps to a tale so truly unbelievable that it must, unbelievably, be true. For it has been said, and it cannot be denied, that strange things can happen when imaginations run wild...

Until next time, until next tale, farewell!

Your servant in storytelling,

—SK

WANT TO FIND OUT ABOUT
SKELETON KEYS' NEXT ADVENTURE:

# THE WILD IMAGININGS
# OF STANLEY STRANGE?

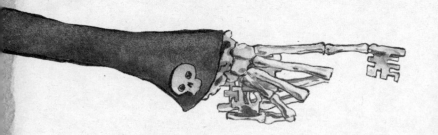

G reetings! To pottlers, do-to-dos and fly-a-ways! To the imaginary and the unimaginary! To the living, the dead and everyone in between, my name is Keys ... Skeleton Keys.

A moon or more ago, before even your wrinkliest relatives were considering being born, I was an IF – an imaginary friend. Then, by a waft of wild imagining, I was suddenly as real as rabbits! I had become unimaginary.

Today, Ol' Mr Keys keeps a watchful eye socket on those IFs who have been recently unimagined. Wherever they appear, so do I! For these fantabulant fingers of mine open doors to anywhere and elsewhere ... hidden worlds ... secret places ... doors to the limitless realm of all imagination. And each door has led to an adventure and then some! The stories I could tell you...

Of course, that is most exactingly why

you are here – for a story. Well, fret not! Here
s a hum-dum-dinger of a tale to send your
brain into a tailspin! A truly unbelievable,
unbelievably true tale I can only call *The Wild
Imaginings of Stanley Strange*.

Stanley imagined his IF five years ago, five
days after his fifth birthday. He named him
Lucky, and the pair of them have been best
friends ever since. Stanley never goes anywhere
without imagining Lucky – and Lucky wants
nothing more than to be Stanley's favourite
figment. Truth be told, Stanley and his IF are
nseparable.

So how is it that Lucky suddenly finds himself
as real as cheese and all alone? How can he be
real if Stanley is nowhere to be found? How can
an IF become unimaginary if there is no one
there to unimagine him? I cannot imagine!

But strange things can happen
when Strange imaginations run wild…

Our story begins upon a hill. The night is dark and there is no shelter from the cold, cruel wind that batters and buffets the land. A lone figure wanders hither and thither, wondering how he came to be there and what became of the boy who imagined him...

Guy Bass is an award-winning author and
semi-professional geek. He has written over thirty books,
including the best-selling *Stitch Head* series (which has been
translated into sixteen languages) *Dinkin Dings and the
Frightening Things* (winner of a 2010 Blue Peter Book Award)
*Spynosaur*, *Laura Norder: Sheriff of Butts Canyon*, *Noah Scape
Can't Stop Repeating Himself*, *Atomic!* and *The Legend of Frog*.

Guy has previously written plays for both adults and children.
He lives in London with his wife and imaginary dog.
Find out more at guybass.com

Pete Williamson is a very self-taught artist and illustrator. He is best known for the much-loved *Stitch Head* and *Skeleton Keys* books by Guy Bass, and the award-winning *The Raven Mysteries* by Marcus Sedgwick.

Pete has illustrated over seventy books by authors including Francesca Simon, Matt Haig, Steve Cole, Robert Louis Stevenson and Charles Dickens.

He now lives at the very edge of a little town in Kent with his family, overlooking a field that he has only just found out might be an ancient burial ground.
Find out more at petewilliamson.co.uk

# Have you read *Stitch Head*?

'It's dark, monstrous fun!' Wondrous Reads

In Castle Grotteskew something BIG
is about to happen to someone SMALL.
Join a mad professor's first creation as
he steps out of the shadows into the
adventure of an almost lifetime...

# Read all Stitch Head's adventures:

# BRINGING THE CHARACTERS TO LIFE

Guy and Pete explain how the characters evolved...

### Flynn

**GB:** I didn't even give Pete a description of Flynn but he nailed his look straight away. He did four sketches with different hairstyles. They could have been plucked straight from my brain.

**PW:** I based Flynn on a friend's son and his fur-collared coat on an old school parka of mine, which always had pockets stuffed full of conkers, crisp packets and bits of paper with doodles on them.

## The Nobody:

**GB:** The Nobody looks like a living shadow with teeth. I did wonder how Pete was going to draw it! He made it genuinely scary. The illustration on pages 14/15 sets the tone for some seriously sinister goings on.

**PW:** I'm glad that, in the end, I didn't have to use the first, more human-shaped, design that I came up with as I think I'd have found illustrating it really unsettling and scary. The one we decided to go with isn't quite as demonic (although I still get a slight shiver down my spine when I see it).

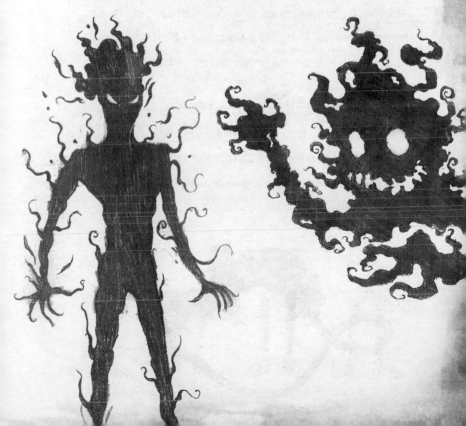

**Fur:**

**GB:** I can't talk about Crystal Fur without mentioning
The Meadow Community Primary School in Leicester.
I had a whale of a time when I visited their school
in early 2020. In assembly, I asked if anyone had an
imaginary friend and their IF's name. From the back of
the hall a girl said, "Crystal Fur" — I thought it was such
a cool name. Crystal Fur! "No," the girl corrected me,
"*Christopher.*" Anyway, the name stuck in my head. I
loved the idea that people would mishear Crystal Fur's
name to Flynn's frustration. So, thanks to everyone at
Meadow Community Primary School! And my poor
hearing, I guess. Pete did a great job of bringing Fur to
life. I love the contrast between her normal form and her
spectacular heroic form.

**PW:** Guy mentioned that Crystal Fur could have an
otter-like face so that led to a pleasant half hour – okay,
afternoon – or so looking at films of otters on the internet
(one more reason why I so often think I have the best job
in the world).

# READ ALL ABOUT SKELETON KEYS' OTHER ADVENTURES...

When Ben's imaginary friend, the Gorblimey, suddenly becomes real, Skeleton Keys is convinced the little monster is dangerous. But someone far more monstrous is out there, waiting to take revenge on Ben...

When Luna's family members start disappearing before her very eyes she thinks her ghostly granddad is to blame. But Skeleton Keys isn't so sure – he's certain something even more mysterious lurks in the shadows – something UNIMAGINARY.

When a dangerous UNIMAGINARY escapes into the past, Skeleton Keys must team up with Gap-tooth Jack to thwart its sinister schemes. But there's something about Jack that is strangely familiar...